Douglas Thayer is a literary treasure. His prose is pitched perfectly between Jack London and Jane Austen—exactly in the Thayer position.

In *Will Wonders Never Cease,* he assumes the voice of a fifteen-year-old boy, Kyle, caught in an avalanche. The reader will chuckle throughout the book as Kyle experiments with words like *worthy, harlot,* and *perish,* but will also feel cold as he assembles his resources and ingenuity to escape the snow.

Inevitably, there will be questions: Will Kyle survive? Will his father get back from his business trip in time to support the family? Will Kyle's mother forgive him for breaking so many rules—particularly the rules Kyle *imagines* he has broken? And this: How can an author in his eighties get a fifte-year-old's voice down so perfectly?

Read this book by a fire, and plan time to savor the wit and word-smithing of a literary master. Give it to a teenage boy, who will be embarrassed but also inspired by how thoroughly he identifies with Kyle.

—Margaret Young
Author, Standing on the Promises trilogy

Will Wonders Never Cease

*A Hopeful Novel for
Mormon Mothers and
Their Teenage Sons*

By Douglas Thayer

Provo, Utah

ISBN 978-0-9883233-2-2

Published by Zarahemla Books
869 East 2680 North
Provo, UT 84604
info@zarahemlabooks.com
ZarahemlaBooks.com

For all Mormon mothers and their Kyles

First Day, Saturday

Standing in the kitchen all dressed to go skiing, I watched Lucille pull out in her new Explorer (which cost Frank a bundle) to go get her hair done. The street was all freshly plowed, the new snow so commodious. I call my mom Lucille and my dad Frank because it's more objective, gives me a chance to study them more, not get so emotional. You have to know what you're doing when it comes to your parents. They can really cause problems if you're not careful. But I'm *very* careful never to call them Frank or Lucille to their faces; Lucille would kill me.

This whole deal was too nefarious. With Lucille gone, I was going skiing *now*. I'd asked her real nice if I could take my Suburban, which Grandpa Hooper left me in his will, but she said no, I'd have to wait for my brother Nate to drive me up the canyon before he went to work later this morning. I told her I'd drive carefully. It's only twelve miles up to Bonanza, the ski resort in Silver Canyon where we have our cabin. I wouldn't get a ticket. I have my learner's permit. No cop was going to pull me over. Sure, I'd got two tickets when I took off in the Suburban and was driving around up Silver Canyon with my friend Mark, being real careful. Old Sheriff Catchwell nailed me both times, and I had to go to juvenile court. Catchwell is always lurking around grabbing kids, like that's all he has to do.

Just twenty-seven more days and I'd turn sixteen and take my driver's test. I'd promised Lucille that when I got back from skiing, I'd write my English paper for old Miss Tolson, the vestal virgin, and do my chemistry and seminary assignments. Seminary. I have to get up an hour early to make seminary five days a week. Give me a break. The maturing Mormon adolescent male needs his sleep; any doctor will tell you that. Recently I made this big effort and went a whole month without being late or missing a class. "Will wonders never cease." That's what Lucille said when I told her, which she always says when I actually get something right.

Today I got up early to clean the foot of new snow off the walks and driveway, even cleaned off old lady Beggar's walks next door, just to soften Lucille up. But I might as well have saved my strength. Lucille's always conning me into cleaning off some lonely widow's driveway or mowing her lawn, says I should be full of charity. Great. I told her that Frank would have let me drive my Suburban just up to Bonanza if he were there, but he was away on a business trip. However, she still said no, especially considering the heavy storm last night and the avalanche danger. I could help her finish putting up the outside lights, and then go with the family to the cabin during Christmas vacation in a couple of weeks and ski as much as I wanted.

Yeah, sure, a delightful Saturday spent at the house with Lucille getting all this work out of me. Just too egregious.

Mark couldn't go skiing today because he had to work. Mark's my best friend. If I waited for my beloved oldest brother Nate to drive over here from his apartment and take me up, the lift lines would be a mile long, and I wouldn't be one of the first to hit all that powder, two feet just lying there. *Lying*, not *laying*. Old Tolson had made us all learn the difference between *lie, lay, lay* and *lay, laid, laid; sit, sat, sat* and *set, set, set;* and *rise, rose, risen* and *raise, raised, raised*—you have to know when you've got a direct object and when you don't. People make that mistake all the time, use the wrong word.

It's so pleasurable to correct them, especially adults, and more especially Lucille. "Don't get smart with me, young man. You know exactly what I mean."

Yeah, sure. Mark is always giving me a hard time about my vocabulary. I just like interesting words. I look them up in the dictionary so I can say them, hear how they sound, and everybody thinks you're so intelligent. Mark's mom is a widow. His dad died when Mark was ten, and he and his mom moved in two houses down from us. Mark never talks about his dad. His mom told Lucille that every time he does he starts to cry, he misses him so much. Mark is already sixteen and drives this old Ford. Mark's not a member. But Lucille's working on him.

One of her six converts was one of Nate's friends, old Melvin Dunker. He went on a mission, got married in the temple, and already has a kid and one more on the way, only it'll probably be triplets, he's so religious. You'd have to be deaf, dumb, and blind not to see that Lucille has her sights on Mark. He has an open invitation to supper when his mom works late, kneels for family prayer, stays for family home evening on Monday nights sometimes. Of course Lucille serves great refreshments afterwards. She'll have him reading scriptures and saying the closing prayer next. I know how she operates. I warned him.

It's so euphoric, skiing deep, new powder, so worthy, everything so white and silent, like you're flying or something. Like your brain's been jerked out and you're all feeling, not thinking about anything, rhythm, doing everything right for once in your life. Just feeling, not thinking, your whole body nothing but feeling, and you want to keep doing that forever and never stop because you're free.

• • •

I got some stuff out of the fridge and put it in the box of groceries that Nate was planning to take to the cabin when he dropped me off. We also had to take up some bananas and oranges to old Mrs. Dyeing, who had a cabin next to ours. She'd phoned Lucille to say she was making this fruit salad for guests and had forgotten the oranges and bananas. Tonight Nate was throwing a party or something up there with some of his pathetic returned-missionary friends and their girls— feeding them hamburgers and hot dogs and all the trimmings, including a big chocolate sheet cake Lucille had made with her great thick frosting. After work, he was planning to pick up some girl and go straight up the canyon. Making these deliveries would save Nate the trip and help convince Lucille how considerate I am, and she wouldn't be so burned at me for taking off.

Nate's been back from his mission four years and isn't married yet. Lucille keeps asking him what else he has to do that's so important. He keeps saying he's working on it. Lucille says to work a little harder. She wants this big herd of grandkids all over the place. My sister, Brooke, is married and going to have a baby, which helps some, I guess. My brother Clay's been back two years and is not married, but that's not so bad as Nate.

We'd dropped Nate and Clay off at the Missionary Training Center in Provo, so I knew all about going on a mission. Your family couldn't even go inside, just had to say goodbye in the parking lot. Moms, little sisters and brothers, even dads crying, the missionary just standing there holding his two suitcases, all dressed in a dark suit. The whole MTC surrounded by an iron fence about ten feet high with a guard station and vehicle barriers, a whole line of missionaries vanishing into the open front doors, the moms waving damp Kleenexes and shouting "Be brave," the dads with their arms around the moms. And the minute you walk through the door you have to put on your missionary tag, like you don't even know you're an elder or your own name or which mission you're going to, or anything.

And if you're going to a foreign-speaking mission like India, Finland, Taiwan, Russia, Romania, Mongolia, or some other wonderful place about a million miles away, you have to study the language for about two months, which Nate and Clay did, ten hours a day, learn all the grammar and vocabulary, and everybody only talks to you in that language. And you have a companion who has to be with you every minute so you won't suddenly take off, and you have to have kneeling prayer every morning and night with him. And you have to keep this journal about all your marvelous spiritual experiences, and bear your testimony to each other all the time. And you have to study the gospel night and day too, memorize all these scriptures. And your branch president has this personal interview with you about three times a day, which is a lot worse than your bishop or stake president, to see if you're developing spiritually. And you have to write home every week and tell your family how wonderful everything is in the good old MTC.

And then after two long, dreary months they load you into a bus and take you to the Salt Lake Airport, and your folks can't even come to say goodbye one more time and maybe cheer you up a little. Your girlfriend, who's promised to wait the whole two years for you, can't come either, to give you a kiss and a hug. Because if she did you'd both be struck dumb probably or turned into pillars of salt like old Lot's wife because she looked back at Sodom, just for a second because she was so sad to be leaving her hometown, which would be perfectly natural.

• • •

I already had my skis on my Suburban, which Lucille says is a wreck to begin with and an eyesore. It's eighteen years old, built like a tank, got two roll bars. I'm lucky to have it. Brooke, Clay, Nate, and Trace, my brother who died, all drove the old family Ford. Once you turned sixteen in our family you had to get a full-time summer job to help pay your own way and start pumping all this money into a mission savings account, especially if you were male, so you didn't have any money for a car. Trace drove the Ford for a year before he got sick, but by then it was a wreck, and Frank gave it to some charity or something.

Sadie came to the kitchen door. She started whining, nuzzling me. She's my dog. "It's okay, girl. You can't go, not this time. I'll be home tonight." I had to push her away with one hand and close the door, heard her scratching and whining like I was never coming back.

I backed out of our driveway slowly, stopped, looked both ways. Sometimes cops are just waiting for you, not out catching real criminals who are killing and raping and robbing people. Cops spend all their time catching fifteen-year-old kids who are safe drivers but just don't have a full license yet.

When Lucille got home and saw my Suburban was gone, she'd really be burned. She'd call me on my phone, but I'd have it turned off, of course. When I finally walked back in the door at six, or maybe even later, if I went over to the lodge to talk to a few lovelies all tired out from skiing, jackets and boots off, just lying back lounging around the fireplace, she'd rip into me. She'd threaten to ground me for six months, take away my allowance, tear up my ski pass, the usual, not let me start dating until I'm twenty and back from my mission. She's always telling me she doesn't expect me to be a spiritual giant but just work on keeping the commandments. I'll be all apologetic, do something nice for her, even do my homework, and she'll be all right. I know how to handle Lucille, get her ruffled feathers all smoothed down. I've had a lot of practice.

But she's tough. Before she married Frank, she'd been a

trauma nurse in a big Denver hospital; she still works part time in the Silver City Hospital emergency room just because she enjoys it so much. She's always telling me about kids coming in with ski injuries, both legs and arms broken, or maybe suffocated from an avalanche, although sometimes kids dig themselves out or the ski patrol finds them in time. If you get buried you have to make a space so you can breathe till the patrol locates you with their long aluminum poles.

When I was twelve, Lucille, not Frank, sat with me through an STD video on the effects of syphilis, gonorrhea, herpes, and AIDS, all in vivid color, all the sores and everything, guys insane because of syphilis, their faces all caved in; poor guys with AIDS, their bodies just like they were rotting. I almost threw up. Nate, Clay, and Trace, before he died, all asked me how I liked Lucille's approach to sex education and then laughed. Very funny. It wouldn't be so bad if Frank had told me all that stuff, or they hit you with it in a health class at school, which they do anyway, but not in living color. Lucille telling me was kind of personal, even if she is a nurse. She's always telling me how sacred the body is.

"Don't think it can't happen to you, buddy." That's what Lucille said. "Any number of smart boys at Jefferson High get an STD, or worse. Brainless wonders."

When I told Mark, he said, "Awesome."

"Yeah, sure, 'awesome.'" Mark's really a great guy. Smart too. Helps me with my trig. He doesn't drink, smoke, use drugs, or *fornicate*, which is a word Lucille uses occasionally when she's talking to me. It's a word I don't like. There ought to be a better word, not so harsh sounding, more mellifluous.

Lucille was even tougher on me after Trace died two years ago. Didn't want me to do anything dangerous, like I could die too or something, like Trace. In addition to all the STD and AIDS stuff, she was always telling me stories about Silver City kids brought into the emergency room dead or dying from drugs, alcohol poisoning, car wrecks, shootings, stabbings, botched abortions, and all kinds of other gross stuff, telling me during supper of course when I'm trying to relax and enjoy myself for maybe five minutes after a hard day at school.

"I lost one son; I don't plan to lose another." She was always pulling that one on me, like I had to stop having any real fun because Trace died. It wasn't my fault. I didn't make him get sick. He was the perfect son—straight 4.0, if you can believe it, state champion tennis player, and a tenor voice like some angel or something, the girls lined up on the front porch or leaving plates of brownies with these notes because he was so cute, so spiritual. I just wanted to live my own life, be myself, not have to worry about what happened to Trace. Lucille really came apart at the seams when Trace died. She cried for a month at least, before she finally got over it. Brooke, my sister who's married to Jed, is going to have a baby boy, which helps some lately.

Lucille is always trying to get me to read the Book of Mormon so I'll get a testimony and know the Church is true. All you have to do is read it and pray about it and you get this big revelation or something. I am reading it. You have to read scriptures every morning before breakfast, even though you're starving, and we are reading it in seminary of course. That ought to be enough. All those *and it came to pass*es get on your nerves. Why did old Mormon have to put those in? Could have saved about fifty pages if he'd left them out.

But Lucille said I have to read it from cover to cover just by myself and pray about whether it's true or not and get a testimony, so I'll know the Church is true for the rest of my life. And I have to keep all the commandments, but I have to have faith too. And then I'll know that Joseph Smith was a prophet and the angel Moroni gave him the gold plates to translate and all that stuff. I can hardly wait.

Of course, going on a mission when you turn eighteen

means you have to keep your nose clean, which is something Grandpa Hooper always said. But your senior year in high school, you really want to have a lot of fun, parties and dances and dating girls all the time, and everything. Just kind of relax after studying so hard all four years, and take off for about a month and drive to California with your buddies for a lot of beach time. But you have to be ready to go on your mission about five minutes after you turn in your graduation hat and gown practically.

So you have to be super righteous, have this big testimony Lucille is always talking about, even when you're a junior, and all the other Mormon guys too, and even the girls because they can go on missions when they're nineteen. Which mean girls are keeping all the commandments in high school, because they are just naturally more spiritual than boys, get all teary-eyed when they bear their testimony in seminary, so how much fun would that be on a date? Miss All Righteous would probably want you to bear your testimony before she'd say she'd go with you to the dance, and to be sure and bring your scriptures.

Lucille was big on the Holy Ghost protecting me and teaching me, if I'd let him, which I do, or thought I did. I was beginning to think about things a lot, what things mean and what kind of a person I was, which Lucille was always telling me to do. So the Holy Ghost was all right with me, especially if he could teach me things like physics and chemistry. I wasn't too worried about the protection; I could take care of myself. I didn't ever get sick. I'd begun to think about God a lot lately too, who he was, where he lived, what he'd do if I didn't keep all the commandments, which I knew was impossible of course, and how he created things.

I don't think about Jesus much. I know about the Atonement and how Jesus paid for our sins, but I don't think I've committed any great sins Jesus has to pay for, as far as I know. I'm interested in having a good time and enjoying myself, which I don't think is any big sin. I know Jesus brought about the resurrection and all that, and I'm glad that Grandpa and Grandma Hooper and Trace will be resurrected, but I figure I have at least about seventy-five or maybe even eighty years left before I'll perish and need to be resurrected or anything, my body all wasted and worn out like Grandpa Hooper, so I don't think about Jesus much. I certainly don't tell Lucille about all this. She'd have a fit, give me a hard time again about my unrepentant soul, whatever that was.

• • •

Driving with my left hand, I took a sucker out of my top parka pocket, unwrapped it, and put in my mouth. Grandpa Hooper liked suckers and was always handing me one, until he died. I liked Grandpa Hooper. He had a lot of great stories to tell. He could really cuss, too, when he really got mad, but nothing obscene. Just good words. Very interesting. I allow myself a *hell* or a *damn* when absolutely necessary. Sometimes something a little more egregious, depending on the circumstances, but I have to watch it around Lucille of course. Grandpa Hooper dropped out of high school and joined the army when he was seventeen, fought in Korea, didn't go on a mission or to college, was a carpenter, electrician, car mechanic. He knew lots of stuff, could do anything, could fix anything, but didn't go to church. He was always telling me that God helps those who help themselves, get the lead out, you have to do your own thinking in this life, and other stuff. Very admirable.

Being careful to drive five miles under the speed limit, watching for old Catchwell and other lurking cops, I got out to Wayne Boulevard and turned east toward the white, beautiful mountains. We'd had over a foot of snow in the valley. The plows had been out. It was a little slick in spots. Taking the sucker out of my mouth, I went into four-wheel drive.

I crossed the beltway and drove into the mouth of Silver Canyon, looking to see if the Forest Service had the barricade up because of the storm. No. Great. I knew they wouldn't. I passed a yellow snowplow working on the shoulder, saw the first sign: "AVALANCHE DANGER—NO STOPPING OR STANDING BETWEEN NOVEMBER 1 AND MAY 1."

I'm planning to try out for the ski patrol next year. It'd be so awesome. Nate had been on the patrol for three years at Bonanza. He told such great stories about digging skiers out of avalanches, mostly dead, but sometimes alive, unconscious, or they dug themselves out if they were only under a foot or two. Or if a car got swept off the road in an avalanche, which happened about once every ten or twenty years, everybody could be alive or dead, depending on whether the car was crushed and if it was only half-buried so they got oxygen. One van was buried ten feet deep but with a huge sheared-off spruce above it sticking out so all six skiers got oxygen and didn't perish.

Ten minutes later I drove out into the two-mile-wide bowl, the plowed snow ten feet deep on each side of the road. Snow-covered Silver Creek at the bottom, the spruce slope on the far side, and the expanse of smooth, untouched powder glistening in the bright morning light, going on forever. The three lifts going up Gold Peak high above everything, all that wonderful powder. So worthy. Another mile and I'd be in the lift parking lot, with maybe only two or three cars ahead of me.

I picked up my phone from the seat and phoned Nate. He didn't answer. I left a message that I'd made it, so I didn't need a ride and to tell Lucille not to worry more than absolutely necessary. I had the food for his party, and I'd take old Mrs. Dyeing her stuff. I turned off the phone and put it back on the seat. I didn't want Lucille calling me and telling me to get my butt home.

Some guy passed me in a big, new blue Suburban, honking his horn, the three passengers at the windows on my side waving, motioning for me to hurry up. I honked, waved, watched them, but I didn't speed up, staying within the speed limit. And then between me and them above the road, I saw this monster whirling, churning cloud of snow rising to hide the clear blue sky.

"What the . . .?"

• • •

I heard myself groaning. My eyes were open, but I couldn't see. I blinked my eyes. Darkness, not just dark but totally dark. I had a terrible headache, felt like I was going to vomit. Where was I? What happened? I touched my lips with my fingers, touched my eyes, pressed my open hand against my face. I couldn't see my hand. I touched the seat belt, knew I wasn't hanging upside down, reached up to touch the roof. It was all dented between the two roll bars. Then I knew. I was under an avalanche—that white, swirling cloud. I was going to suffocate, die as soon as the oxygen ran out, maybe five minutes, maybe less.

I screamed, not words, just screaming, terrible sounds I'd never made in my whole life before. I stopped, took shallow breaths, knew I was going to die. I'd soon start gasping for breath, put my hands up to my throat just like in this flick I saw once. Still breathing shallow, trying not to scream, my arms tight around my chest, I waited, scared of what it would feel like to die, afraid I would wet my pants.

Would I just suddenly not be a person anymore, lose my body, be a spirit floating around or something, end up in the spirit world, wherever that was, like old Brother Glimmer was always telling us in seminary? Be something invisible you couldn't see or touch, like gas or vapor, maybe kind of evaporate? I couldn't not have my body and still be me. How could I drive my own car, go skiing, be with girls, take long, hot showers, eat pizza, play video games, get married, go on a honeymoon for at least a month, without one? Not having a body would be too horrendous.

"I don't want to die. Don't want to die. Not me. Please, God." Whispering, reaching out in the darkness, I touched the steering wheel, grabbed it, rocked back and forth, started pounding on it. "Please, God, please."

I stopped. I'd heard the horn. I knew I had. I pushed the horn, kept doing that. I couldn't believe it. I still had battery power. Grandpa Hooper always said the Suburban was built like a tank. I kept pushing the horn. I stopped. I reached out and turned the headlight switch. The ceiling and dashboard lights came on. I could see. I could see. I could see. I saw my breath.

"Oh, thank you, God. Thank you."

I turned around. The back ceiling light was out. The plastic cover was broken. Something had hit it. But at least I had one ceiling light.

I leaned forward. Two o'clock. The dashboard clock said two o'clock. I'd been buried for almost six hours, not just maybe three or four minutes. I'd been out that long. I was getting air somehow. I wasn't going to die.

The Suburban wasn't buried, just sitting on top somewhere, maybe half sticking out. Nate had never had to dig out a car, but he told me ski-patrol stories he'd heard about cars being hit by an avalanche, sometimes a car lifted by the hundred-and-fifty-mile-an-hour winds and set right down on top like a basket of eggs, and nobody hurt. But mostly the ski patrol found everybody inside dead of asphyxiation, all of them just sitting there in their ski hats and parkas strapped in under twenty feet of snow, or everybody was crushed, which was what happened most of the time. I figured the Suburban was sticking half out or was maybe only ten feet down under a big spruce. I honked the horn, turning the headlights on and off, signaling, but then I stopped.

The ski patrol should have found me by now if the Suburban was only half-buried, the top showing, or maybe the front or back half sticking out. It'd been six hours. "Where are you guys?" They formed lines, got skiers to help, and kept pushing these long aluminum poles down into the snow to try and find bodies or maybe a car, if one ever got knocked off the road. But maybe the avalanche was so deep the poles weren't long enough or so big, a mile long and two hundred yards across, that it took a long time. But I was getting air. They had to be able to see the Suburban, hear me honking, or see the lights going on and off.

They had to know I got hit. The people in the blue Suburban ahead of me would tell them that. And when the avalanche came down, even though it was almost a mile away across the basin, skiers at the lift and in the parking lot would have heard it, turned to see it sweep me off the road, bury me.

The windshield was smashed, half pushed in. I turned. All the doors were bent in, the windows bulged, both rear windows all smashed in so snow came in, the box of groceries all scattered. The two roll bars had helped save me, that and the Suburban being so big and heavy. "Thanks, Grandpa." So gratifying.

I had to tap a kidney, an expression I picked up from Grandpa. I crawled over the seat in back. Grandpa Hooper had taken out the other seat so he could haul lumber and other stuff. I tried not to step on the scattered groceries.

Where the snow came was a good place. The end of Grandpa Hooper's toolbox stuck out of the snow. He'd bolted it to the floor, with a clip through the hasp so the lid wouldn't fly open. If the toolbox had hit me in the head, it really would have been the bitter end. I pounded on the windows, but the snow didn't slide off, so I probably wasn't on top. I checked the back ceiling light. The globe was broken, the socket bent. Too bad. The quilt Grandpa Hooper always had in the Suburban, which Grandma Hooper had made, lay between the front and back seats. I grabbed that.

My fingers were getting numb. I found my gloves on the floor. I zipped up my parka, pulled the hood over my hat, and put on my gloves. I spread out the quilt on the seat, sat down, and wrapped up in it. Leaning forward, I looked in the rearview mirror, my face like a shadow. Dried blood ran all the way down the side of my face where something had cracked me on the head.

I honked the horn and turned the headlights on and off three times to signal just in case, because three times meant you needed help. I wanted to turn on the radio and start the engine to see if the heater worked. I looked at the keys. They were turned off. I must have done that. I couldn't remember. I must have. But even if I could start the engine, the exhaust would kill me. I had to save the battery for the overhead lights. I had to be able to see.

They should have found me by now, seen the lights, heard the horn.

"You idiot." I sat straight up in the seat.

My phone. I'd just call 911, tell them where I was and that I was still alive. It would work. I called girls from our basement family room all the time when Mark and I were supposed to be down there studying. I called them while I was skiing. I liked to tell them what it felt like and tell them I wished they were there because it was so transcendent.

"Idiot."

I got the flashlight out of the glove compartment. I found my phone on the floor all dented.

"Oh, no, no. Damn." I'd stepped on it.

I opened it. No light, no signal. "Damn."

Holding the phone, I sat back in the seat, not believing the phone was broken, feeling all empty inside. How could it be broken? It wasn't fair.

If it had worked, I could have called Lucille, and she wouldn't believe me of course, and she'd nail me for taking off in the Suburban and tell me there'd be a slight delay of about six months in getting my driver's license, that I could forget about skiing the whole holiday because I'd be spending most of my time studying and practicing the piano and stuff like that, which she always said. I'd call Mark, who wouldn't believe me and would ask me if I knew anymore bedtime stories, which he always said. I'd say it was so worthy, and he'd say, "What do you mean *worthy*. You're always saying that." And I'd tell him again it was a word I liked and he'd say, "You and your words."

I'd call Summer Landers, so hot, a real lovely. She'd believe me, her voice all choky. She'd say, "Oh, Kyle, you're so brave."

I haven't dated Summer yet, because Lucille won't let me date till I'm sixteen. Even then I can't date the same girl more than three times in a row, which is pretty lame, like I'd be sleeping with her after the first date and get her pregnant or something. So pathetic. How could you really get to know a girl and have her like you the way she should unless you dated just her?

But Summer and I have hung out a lot together with the other guys. Summer is really classy, great shape, lots of fun, smart, can really ski. I want to have her be my girlfriend after I'm sixteen and not go out with any other guys, just be mine to kiss good night on the lips on her porch with the light on because Lucille said that's all the kissing I needed to do until I got back from my mission and it meant something. And hold hands with her and put my arms around her sitting on her sofa in front of her fireplace, watching the flames, all red and warm. And just stand there in the hall at school, tell her how worthy she is, but mostly just to be with her and talk about things. Summer's a member, really loves the gospel, goes to seminary and everything. This cheers up Lucille considerably, who knows the Church is true of course, has this big testimony, and is always on my case to keep the commandments, as if that's all I have to think about in my difficult life.

• • •

My feet were getting numb. I found my racked ski boots and put them on They were awkward to move in but warmer than my shoes.

I turned off the ceiling light and the flashlight. I put my hand up to my face again, pressed, but I couldn't see it, like I didn't have eyes, or even a body. Like I was just a brain. I counted out loud to a hundred just to hear my voice. I still couldn't figure out how I was getting air. I had to be close to the surface, air getting to me somehow. I just had to be.

I felt sorry for my family when they heard I was dead, all my uncles and aunts and cousins, felt sorry for everybody at school too, Mark, the girls I knew, even old Tolson, who sort of likes me. I thought about my funeral, and how sad Lucille would be sitting there looking at my casket up in front of the podium, just like Trace's, but me in it this time, wishing she'd always been kind and generous to me, now that it was too late of course.

Sitting there not being able to see a thing, not even my nose, I felt the corners of my eyes fill with tears. But I wasn't really crying, just very sad.

At school on Monday they would make the announcement over the loudspeakers that Kyle Frank Hooper was dead. Principal Jagger would make the announcement, which he always did when it was serious.

"Silver High students, good morning. This is Principal Jagger. I'm very sorry, but I'm afraid I have some tragic news, very tragic. As some of you undoubtedly already know, one of our wonderful students, Kyle Hooper, was killed in an avalanche in Silver Canyon Saturday. I know this is a terrible shock to us all. Kyle was a fine young man and a splendid student. He will be greatly missed. Grief counselors will be working with those who were taking classes with Kyle to help you in this great loss. Please be patient and go on with your studies."

The girls in my classes, especially Summer, would start to cry like they did when Jeff Biller OD'd, not real crying but their eyes all shiny with tears. Mark would be very sad too. He was such a cool guy. Rob Turner, Chris Monson, Dave Wilkins, Jesse Crowe, and the other guys in our crowd would be sad too.

I closed my eyes because there wasn't any point in keeping them open in the darkness. The more I thought about how sad everybody was going to be about me being dead, especially Lucille, the worse I felt. I blinked my eyes against the tears and wiped them away with the back of my glove, but I still wasn't crying. I felt sadder and sorrier for myself than anybody else would feel for me. I thought about getting the pencil out of the jockey box and writing a long letter on a piece of cardboard telling everybody how sorry I was to have to die, and even telling Lucille I wished I'd done all those things she wanted me to do. I wondered if they had houses in heaven and if you had to keep your room clean, do your own washing and ironing, mow the lawn, shovel snow, have homework, practice the piano, only it would probably be a harp, and all that stuff. But heaven had to be more fun than that, didn't it, or how could it be heaven?

Sitting there I thought about Trace dying. He stopped going to school, and went to see a lot of doctors. He had all these tests, and then he was in bed all the time, getting thinner and weaker. And Nate, Clay, Jed, Bishop Goodmer, and President Smyles, who was the stake president, came, and Frank, who was voice, all of us in the bedroom, gave Trace a blessing. But Frank didn't tell Trace to rise up from his bed of affliction and walk. Frank just gave him a blessing of comfort and told him to have faith and accept the Lord's will. They came and blessed Trace twice more, President Smyles once and Bishop Goodmer once, but they didn't say Trace would be healed. The whole ward fasted and prayed for him. Lucille just shook her head and cried but told us we had to accept the Lord's will. Lucille has a lot of faith, I guess, whatever that is supposed to mean.

And there was nothing else the doctors could do because the disease was so complicated and advanced. And about a dozen knock-out girls came to visit Trace, real lovelies, and they brought brownies and cookies, and stood around saying, "You're so brave, so wonderful. We just know you're going to get all better." And Trace just lay there in bed in his pajamas, blanket pulled up to his chest, thanking them, smiling faintly, pale, and looking tragic and heroic at the same time. Laura Loveland, this really classy blonde with lips worth marrying for, whom Trace liked the best, came to visit just by herself. Walking down the hall I'd see her sitting on the edge of Trace's bed holding both his hands in hers.

Obviously I couldn't tell Lucille because I knew what she'd say, but it would be so awesome if everybody thought you were dying; they'd be so sad and tell you what a wonderful person you were, especially all these girls. And then you'd get a priesthood blessing or something and have so much faith you'd be healed instantly because you were so righteous. And you'd stand up right out of bed like in the pioneer stories Brother Glimmer was always feeding us in seminary, and they'd go off on a mission for about ten years, leaving their wife and nine kids. And everybody would be so grateful and happy you didn't perish, especially your parents, who'd buy you a new car or something. And all the girls would be so nice to you because you nearly died.

And I figured that was what would happen to Trace, because he couldn't die, not really; he was too young and super righteous. Grandpa Hooper had died, but he was old, which is when people died mostly, except for accidents and drugs and things. Trace wasn't old.

But then Trace died. He went into a coma and died early on Friday evening, March twenty-fifth, two years ago, everybody there except Frank, who was on a business trip to New York. Trace's eyes were closed. He didn't say goodbye, or how much he loved everybody, or anything, which they do in the movies, which you'd kind of expect.

"My beautiful son. My beautiful, beautiful son." Saying that, Lucille sat on the edge of the bed smoothing back Trace's hair.

I just stood there looking at Trace, his eyes closed, lying there, just like when he was asleep, his face pale and thin, his arms outside the covers, except he was dead. I didn't cry. I had this funny empty feeling, but I didn't cry. I still couldn't believe it. I didn't know it was so easy to die. Jed had his arm around Brooke, who had an arm around Lucille, and they were both crying. Nate and Clay were just standing there like they were statues or something.

We all knelt around his bed and Nate said a prayer. The people from Crane's Funeral Home came and got Trace and put him on a gurney, covered him with a blanket, and took him down the stairs and out the front door and loaded him in their black hearse. Neighbors stood watching, their arms around their kids, like they were protecting them or something. And then the neighbors started coming over, the women hugging Lucille. And they came back later bringing lots of good food. And the bishopric came, then the stake president and a counselor, and lots of ward members bringing food, the house crowded with people.

Later, standing in the hall outside Lucille and Frank's bedroom, I heard Lucille talking to Frank on the phone, telling him Trace was dead and he should be there, not in New York.

"Oh, what difference does it make? You'll never understand. We'll pick you up at the airport. Maybe someday you'll figure out what's really important and how much you're needed, but I doubt it. Try to make it for your son's funeral, if you're not too busy."

• • •

Leaning forward, feeling with my hands, I pulled the quilt tighter around myself against the cold, folded my arms tight against my chest under it. I didn't open my eyes. What was the point?

After Trace died, I thought it would be really radical if every ward had one resurrected person in it who could tell everybody what it was like to die and then be resurrected. Lucille could go talk to this person, and learn all the details about the Atonement, the three degrees of glory, the resurrection, all this other stuff she was so interested in, like genealogy, and what Trace was doing in heaven, which would make her feel better. I thought about telling Lucille my resurrected-ward-member idea, but then decided not to. I knew what she'd do, shake her head, and say, "I pray on my knees morning and night for strength."

I opened my eyes and then closed them again. I didn't like not seeing. Being buried inside the Suburban was like being in a cave. Grandpa Hooper told me about an Air Force colonel he'd read about who had been shot down over Vietnam and captured. He'd spent six years in a bamboo cage so small he couldn't stand up in it.

"Six years, Kyle, six years. Think about that. Lost ninety pounds, had boils, sores, dysentery, some of his teeth fell out. But they never broke him. Damn it, that's a real man for you. When he got home the Air Force made him a general."

My eyes still closed, I listened for an aluminum pole to clunk against the roof of the buried Suburban.

I knew Lucille would have the whole ward praying for me once she knew I was in the avalanche, the whole stake if she could arrange it. She was a great believer in prayer. She said she needed all the help she could get raising me. "Brainless wonder" was her favorite name for me, but she also liked "Romeo," "party boy," "Mr. Cool," "hot shot," "Tarzan," and a few others, depending on the mood she was in.

Lucille was always bearing her testimony on fast Sunday, saying how much she loved the Church and wanted her family to keep the commandments because that was the only way to find happiness in this life or the life to come, which she was always preaching to me about. Keep the commandments, keep the commandments. How was I supposed to do that every minute of my life, not ever do anything wrong, start being all spiritual like Trace, whatever that was supposed to mean? Frank would pat Lucille on the shoulder (if he was in town) when she sat down after her testimony; he never bore his except about once every five years.

And I knew Lucille was just sitting there in fast and testimony meeting waiting for me to stand up and walk to the podium and bear my testimony, which I hadn't done yet. Because if you bore your testimony and said you knew the Church was true, all the ward members, especially your Primary, Varsity, and priesthood leaders, knew all their efforts hadn't been wasted and you weren't a total screw-up after all, and you'd probably even go on a mission. And at the end of the meeting they'd come up and shake your hand, even hug you, the old sisters kissing you on the cheek, they'd be so happy for your eternal soul, and you'd have to start being super righteous, which didn't seem a particularly interesting way to spend your young life.

And I didn't know the Church was true anyway, at least not yet, not really, not like Trace, who was always bearing his testimony, was president of his seminary class two years straight, although I was working on it, of course. Old Frank would be happy too if I did and put his arm around me when I sat back down, Lucille just sitting there with tears in her eyes, she'd be so grateful. Except Frank was gone so often on business trips that he might not make that fast and testimony meeting. The only priesthood responsibility he had in the ward was home teacher, with me as his companion, which was okay except he liked to stay and talk to people. He'd never been a bishop or anything like that, not even a counselor.

• • •

I opened my eyes. Darkness. It was like I was totally blind. I hugged myself to stop the shivering. I was surprised at how hungry I was. I hadn't even thought about food until then. I turned on the dash and ceiling lights, saw my breath, the windshield frosty on the inside. Three o'clock. I'd been in the avalanche seven hours. I was still getting air.

I got up and put all the food and stuff back in the cardboard box. The big can of pork and beans was under the front seat. It had dried blood on it.

"So that's what hit me on the head."

The bag of potato chips was broken, the chips scattered all over, all wet and soggy and sort of melted. I found the chocolate cake under the seat, broken in about ten pieces, but not dumped out because the pan had one of those slide-on clear plastic lids. Very gratifying. I picked up the new roll of heavy-duty aluminum foil. The bananas and oranges were bruised, but I put them in the box. The gallon of milk had popped the lid and spilled. I had plenty of food even if it took the ski patrol until tomorrow to find me. Grandpa's toolbox hadn't sprung open because of the clip through the hasp. He was so smart to bolt it to the floor.

"Thanks, Grandpa."

Wrapped up in the quilt, just my hands free, gloves off, in the dim light I made myself two icy hotdogs with plenty of mustard and catsup. I put them on a paper plate next to me on the seat with a big piece of chocolate cake, and popped open a can of Coke.

I'd read about mountain climbers digging snow caves and surviving for days in terrible storms, winds over a hundred miles an hour, the temperature fifty degrees below. I knew the thing I had to worry about was hypothermia and frostbite, not freezing to death, at least for now.

• • •

After I ate, I turned off the dash and overhead lights again, lay back in the reclined seat, wrapped tight in the quilt, and closed my eyes.

They'd know I was in the avalanche, and they'd have the ski patrol and skiers out looking for me, long lines of them with aluminum poles. Lucille would keep calling me, and she'd have her little TV on in the kitchen, and she'd hear this announcement that an old red Suburban had been hit by an avalanche at Bonanza early that morning, or maybe Nate would hear it, or Mark, or Brooke, or somebody, and they'd know it was me. Nate would rush to the house and hug Lucille and tell her there wasn't any hope because the Suburban would be crushed flat, I'd been buried for hours, and even if by some miracle I'd survived I'd have suffocated because I couldn't possibly get oxygen for that long.

And Lucille would say, "I won't let Kyle be dead. I've lost one son. I won't lose another one. I won't. God won't let that happen."

"Mom, you've got to be sensible."

"No I don't. No I don't."

Lucille would call Frank, who would be on the next plane

for Silver City. Nate, Clay, and Brooke and her husband Jed would be at the house when they heard I was dead, the house crowded with relatives and neighbors, Bishop Goodmer and probably President Smyles, just like when Trace died, people bringing all this good food. Mark and his mom would come, and my other friends. Summer would come and all the girls from school who liked me a lot. They'd stand around, their eyes shiny with tears, telling each other what a great person I was, just like Trace's friends did when he died. Sadie would whine, people reaching down to pet her. And Sunday morning, ward members, all my friends from high school, and our neighbors who could ski would be up joining in the search. We had great neighbors; we were the only Mormon family on the whole block, both sides. My picture would be on TV Sunday with the story about how I was tragically killed in the avalanche.

Suddenly without even thinking about it, I said, "Help me, God, to get home. Please help me. Bless my family and everybody so they don't worry so much. And thanks a lot for the air so I didn't have to die or anything."

It wasn't a prayer. I didn't say amen and I didn't say in the name of Jesus Christ either, like Lucille taught me to when she knelt by my bed with me until I was seven or eight. Lucille was always telling me to say my prayers and ask for the Holy Ghost to guide me because if anybody needed help, I did, and to start using my head a little bit because I was old enough. I prayed sometimes, not kneeling because that was kind of embarrassing, but lying in bed under the covers just thinking about God mostly, or Jesus, which I decided was praying, sort of. I didn't really have Jesus figured out yet. I knew he was my brother and had been crucified and rose from the dead and all that, but I didn't know how he could pay for everybody's sins and a lot of other stuff, but it sounded like a good idea.

I just needed help not to die, and God was the only one

I could think of asking, except maybe Grandpa Hooper. I didn't know exactly how dead people could help you, but I figured they could if they were alive somewhere and knew what was happening. And maybe Trace could help me too somehow. Sitting there in the darkness, not knowing whether my eyes were closed or open, I watched for some ski-patrol guy to scrape a window clean of snow, shine his flashlight, look in, and yell, "Anybody still alive in there?" Even if it was night maybe they were searching with flashlights and flares; maybe they thought the Suburban might be just half-buried or something.

Sitting there I thought about Lucille. I didn't want her to worry and be sad about me like she was about Trace because I was dead too.

Second Day, Sunday

I opened my eyes. I couldn't see. At first I didn't know where I was. I'd been dreaming about being home. I was just coming in the front door from school after Mark dropped me off.

"Is that you, Kyle?" Lucille always said that.

"No, it's Batman"—or maybe Jack the Ripper. I always wanted to say that. But I didn't. Lucille didn't like a smart mouth.

I was cold, my feet a little numb. My head still hurt. It was like I'd been born without eyes. Not just blind but without eyes, just bone, flesh, and skin where my eyes should have been so I wasn't even sensitive to light. In biology we'd studied about fish and salamanders that lived in pools in deep caves and didn't have any eyes because of evolution.

I turned on the dash and ceiling lights and then pulled the quilt even tighter around myself. I looked at the dash clock. Eight-twenty. I'd been in the avalanche a whole day.

I still wasn't freezing, was still getting air. I opened the quilt and took off my gloves to look at my fingers. The tips hadn't turned white. Because there were so many skiers and snowboarders at Jefferson High School, every November the health classes spent a whole class period studying about hypothermia and frostbite and how to recognize and prevent them. Two paramedics came from one of the Silver City fire stations to show a film and lead a discussion. I knew I'd have to be careful and rub my hands and feet when they got cold. I didn't want my finger and toes to turn black and have to be cut off when I got out, which would be sort of detrimental. The whole inside of the Suburban was white with a thin frost. I knew it was from my breath. The paramedics said that snow was a good insulation; if you got lost in the mountains in the winter you could dig a snow cave.

They told us that when you froze to death, your hands and feet froze first and then your arms and legs, the cold moving into the center of your body until your core temperature dropped so low that first you went all comatose and then you were dead. Sitting in class watching the film, I'd wondered if your brain froze before your heart, blood, eyes, lungs, kidneys, liver, and bladder. But I didn't think so. If your brain froze first then you wouldn't be able to tell about the other things freezing, especially your bladder. I asked Mark about that after class.

"Hooper, you're nuts."

"I know, but people wonder about things like that. It's worthy."

"No, they don't. Just you."

"I should have asked about it."

"Oh, sure. Give me a break, Hooper. Every kid in the class would have thrown a book at you, especially the girls."

But I did wonder. Like Lucille said, I'd really begun to think a lot about who I was and my body and things. I just really started liking myself and thinking about that. I liked my body and my brain and that I was a person. I liked to watch myself. I'd look at myself standing in front of my full-length mirror drying off after my shower or all dressed for church in my tie, white shirt, suit, and polished black shoes, my hair combed just right. I kept turning, really looking at myself. I liked to walk past big mirrors just to see my body moving. I'd just hold out my hands to look at them and think about what they'd done or could do.

I didn't tell anybody except Mark because he said he did it too, and we talked about that sometimes. But we didn't tell each other everything because we didn't know everything about ourselves, at least not yet, and some things are too personal and important anyway. I wanted somebody to take a DVD of me running track, skiing, swimming, riding my mountain bike, sitting in church or class, dancing with some really hot lovely, or just sleeping so I could watch it on TV and see myself whenever I wanted. And I wanted DVDs of back when I was just born so I could see myself, see how much I'd changed on my birthday every year. It would be very educational.

I turned off the lights and sat back, closed my eyes. I knew they'd be searching for me even though they'd think I was dead, all my friends from school, the neighbors, and members from the ward in long lines pushing the long aluminum poles down into the avalanche. I kept listening. Nate had told me they searched for three or four days just to find one dead body, but sometimes they didn't find it even then because the person was buried too deep, and the family had to wait until the spring thaw melted the snow.

I thought if they had a metal detector or some kind of imaging machine, they could locate the Suburban with that. But then I remembered that the bowl was strewn with old rusted boilers, big solid rubber-tired trucks, bulldozers, diesel engines, ore cars, and sections of railroad tracks from the abandoned gold and silver mines. Mark and I used to hike out into the bowl in the summer from the cabin to play in the old equipment. They'd never detect the Suburban. The ski patrol would have to dig about a hundred holes before they found me. It'd take all winter, and avalanches moved things around anyway, so they couldn't be sure. They'd just figure I was dead, so what was the point? Just wait till the spring melt, and there I'd be all thawed out and ready to go. It made me feel strange knowing people thought I was dead already, which I wasn't. Not very copacetic.

I knew a TV crew would be up shooting the avalanche the minute the road was cleared. They'd shoot Lucille, Frank, Nate, Clay, and Brooke and Jed parked up by the bowl watching the lines of searchers pushing their poles in and pulling them out. Even though it was Sunday, ward members and neighbors would be in the line. The TV crew would have my picture and show that. I knew that Lucille would stay all day. Lucille had faith. She'd have everybody praying for me.

I had to go tap a kidney again. I turned on the ceiling light. While I was in the back, I realized how hungry I was again. It was ten o'clock. I studied the food in the box. I tossed the package of frozen hamburger in the back; I wouldn't be devouring any raw hamburger, that's for sure. I got three hot dogs and three buns, a dented orange, a big piece of Lucille's chocolate cake, and a can of Pepsi and crawled back to my seat and wrapped up in the quilt. I had plenty of food.

"Get your butt in gear and get to work, Kyle." I knew that's what Grandpa Hooper would say. "God helps those who help themselves. Don't just sit around feeling sorry for yourself. Start digging yourself out, Kyle."

But how could I do that? I could be under thirty feet of snow, even more. It was impossible. I was trapped. I was going to run out of air, die a sad, lingering death, or something worse, if they didn't find me, which I knew they probably wouldn't.

Grandpa Hooper had a shop where he built and repaired things, and taught me how to use all these tools. He skied, played the banjo, and knew all these great songs. He showed us how to build the cabin. It took four summers. Frank didn't help much because he was always away on business trips. Although Lucille didn't like Grandpa Hooper's swearing and not going to church, she gave him credit for teaching me how to work and teaching me the names of all the plants, trees, and birds and animals in the canyon.

Grandpa Hooper always had stories to tell about fighting forest fires, mining for gold, catching crooks when he was a sheriff's deputy, and hunting bears and mountain lions, which Mark liked to listen to too. He wished he had a grandpa who'd had such an interesting life. Grandpa Hooper had been a sergeant and won medals and been wounded. I just wished Frank had done things like that.

• • •

I honked the horn three more times, stopped, and then honked it again. I turned the headlights off and on three times, and then turned off the ceiling light. I had to save the battery. I kept shivering. I just wished I could turn on the heater. It would be so great to be warm.

I really wished Mark had come with me. That would be so euphoric. We'd both be heroes. The girls would go crazy. But then I didn't want anything bad to happen to Mark.

I knew I really had to think, to figure things out, how I was still getting air. Maybe the snow above the Suburban was only fifteen feet deep but with a big spruce on top that blocked the aluminum poles. But if there was another avalanche, it could cut off my air, and I'd really be toast. Or maybe a big storm would drop three or four feet of snow. Maybe I really was going to have to dig myself out, or just maybe perish.

"Hardest thing in the world, Kyle, is to think and have faith in yourself," Grandpa always said. "You got to learn to use your head if you want to be a man. People don't like to think. It takes time. You don't always like what you find out about yourself. You just have to learn to do the best you can— just don't turn into a whiner or a bellyacher."

Resources. I had to look at my resources, what I had to work with inside the Suburban. Grandpa Hooper was always talking about resources. If Mark were here he'd help me figure things out. He's smart.

I guess it was my fault that Lucille started working on Mark, getting him interested in the Church and being baptized and going to the celestial kingdom. I certainly didn't mean to. Mark didn't play on the Silver High varsity basketball team, but he had a great outside shot, and I asked him to come and play on our ward team. And when Lucille heard that he was playing and I'd invited him, she said, "How nice, Kyle. You surprise me sometimes." Like I was trying to convert him or something. Brother.

Lucille started bringing cookies after every game and talking to Mark. And then she invited him to firesides, telling him about the refreshments, and to ward parties and suppers. And you'd have to be deaf, dumb, and blind not to see what she was up to. She introduced Mark to Bishop Goodmer, who of course shook his hand and told him what a fine-looking young man he was and that he was always welcome to meetings and all the ward activities. And ward members, especially the older sisters, told him how welcome he was, insisting that he have a second dish of chocolate cake and ice cream. I warned Mark that they were all in on it, and they'd be dunking him soon, but it didn't do any good.

"People are nice to me. I enjoy coming. The firesides are interesting. They make you think about who you are and about God and eternity and everything. You call each other brother and sister. The other youth activities are great. The refreshments are sure good, and you have those great ward suppers."

"Yeah, bait for the trap. Bishop Goodmer will have you in for a baptism interview next. And Lucille will be working on me to be a better example for you."

"Well, you're not perfect yet. You've still got a few minor flaws you might want to work on."

"Not perfect yet? Don't give me that stuff. You're worse than Lucille. I thought you were my friend."

"I am. I have your welfare at heart."

"Oh, sure."

• • •

Wrapped in the quilt in the darkness, I felt I might start screaming again, but if I did that I might never stop. I might start bawling and eat all the chocolate cake and drink all my pop, just give up and not care about anything because I'd be dead when the ski patrol found me anyway.

So noxious. Lucille would be so sad; I really felt sorry for her because Trace had already died on her. She'd bury me out there in the Silver City cemetery next to Trace and Grandma and Grandpa Hooper with my name and dates on the headstone. She'd put "Beloved, Blessed Son" on Trace's headstone; I wondered what she'd come up with for mine. Probably "He Often Meant Well," or something else equally gratifying.

But I knew I couldn't just give up. I had to at least try. What if I met Grandpa Hooper in heaven or some other place? He'd just look at me and shake his head. He couldn't stand a quitter.

I pushed back the quilt, turned on the light, and looked around. First I'd have to get outside of the Suburban to start digging a shaft. How was I going to do that? I couldn't open a door or even climb out a window. Anyway, the avalanche would probably cave in on me once I started to dig, if I ever did. All the light I had for digging was the flashlight, the extra batteries, and a candle in the toolbox. I looked around. The passenger window was the best one to go out of, but it was kind of bent. How was I supposed to fix that? What was I going to do with the snow even if I could get a shaft started? I would just have to throw it in the back of the Suburban till I filled it up. I didn't know what I'd do after that.

Grandpa Hooper told me once about an American climber in Switzerland years ago who fell into a huge crevasse in a glacier. His wife had a scientist figure out how fast the glacier was moving and how long it would take for the body to come out.

"She was waiting right there for him, Kyle, sixty years later, and there he was, frozen, looked like he did the day he fell in. His wife was almost ninety. She had a funeral for him and buried him right there in that Swiss village. She'd never remarried. Just waited for him to show up. Son, that's what you call loyalty."

I liked the story, but what I really wanted to hear was some of Grandpa's Korean War stories about bayonet charges, throwing hand grenades, firing machine guns, being a sniper using a scope-sighted rifle, and things like that. Grandpa Hooper had been wounded in the chest. I wanted to know what it was like lying there with a hole in you, bleeding, and one of your buddies yelling, "Medic! Medic!" And then spending two months in a hospital in Japan with the nurses and doctors and everybody taking care of you because you'd been such a hero and won some big medal. But Grandpa Hooper wouldn't tell me. He said I should be grateful I didn't have to fight in a war.

Of course, Lucille was always telling me how grateful I should be, and that I had everything a fifteen-year-old boy could want.

"Oh, sure. I can think of a few things I'd like to have."

"Like what for heaven's sake?"

"How about a new red Jaguar convertible just for starters."

"Be sensible."

"I am being sensible—for a fifteen-year-old."

"I hope not. You're not fifteen; you're almost sixteen."

"You asked me."

"Oh, go practice the piano."

"Go practice the piano. Go practice the piano. I live a very difficult life."

"You don't know what the word means."

"I'm learning."

• • •

Holding the flashlight, I checked every part of the Suburban. I thought of an old flick Mark and I saw called *The Count of Monte Cristo*. This old prisoner who knew all about this treasure buried on an island had spent twenty years cutting a tunnel through solid rock and had come up in this other prisoner's cell and not through the outside wall. But he didn't get mad or discouraged; he was glad for the company.

The flashlight beam hit the jack bolted to the side of the Suburban. The plastic cover had fallen off. I kept looking at it. I remembered when we were building the cabin, Grandpa Hooper had used the jack to push some of the bottom cabin logs a couple of inches into place. He'd braced the jack against the bumper of the Suburban.

"Wake up, bright boy."

I could use the jack to pry open the passenger window. I swallowed hard. I still had a chance. So portentous. Bolted next to the jack was Grandpa's trenching tool with a fold-up blade like soldiers used in wars to dig fox holes, as well as a small bow saw. I could use the trenching tool to shovel snow and the saw to cut limbs.

"Thanks again, Grandpa."

I thought maybe the Holy Ghost had helped me too; that's what he was for, partly anyway. But I knew I had to use my head too, or I didn't have a snowball's chance in hell, which

was something Grandpa Hooper always said, that and hot as
the hinges of hell, which I liked to hear him say too. He had a
very interesting vocabulary. I looked at the dashboard clock.
Two in the afternoon, Sunday. The ski patrol would still be
looking for me, the long lines of searchers with their aluminum
poles spread out across the avalanche.

I kept thinking about Lucille. She had all these stories
about people with great faith she was always telling me, the
Holy Ghost protecting and guiding them if they were super
righteous. Like Daniel and the tame lions, the three guys in the
fiery furnace in the Bible, and the sons of Mosiah, and of course
the stripling warriors in the Book of Mormon. Lucille was big
on Helaman and his warriors, who were such a wonderful
example and were probably just sixteen or seventeen, so why
couldn't I be a little bit like them, so brave and full of faith? Oh
sure. They got wounded and lost all that blood, but never died
because they had all this faith. I knew faith was important, but
I didn't really understand what it was, maybe like gravity or
something or doing things and not knowing why but knowing
they'd turn out all right in maybe fifty years.

Standing by the car watching the lines of searchers with
their aluminum poles, Frank would put his arms around
Lucille to hold her tight. Nate would say, "Mom, Kyle's been
in the avalanche for over thirty hours. They're not going to
find him alive. Everybody knows that. Sheriff Catchwell told
us that yesterday." Nate would shake his head. "You've got to
be reasonable. You have to accept that. I was on ski patrol for
three years. I dug dead people out."

"I've already lost one son. I don't want to be reasonable."

"Mom."

I could have told them all about Lucille being reasonable.
Bishop Goodmer and the other two bishops in our building
asked her, because she was a nurse and was always talking
in Relief Society about the need for sex education in Church

families, to do a PowerPoint sex-education presentation for the three wards. Bishop Goodmer would narrate it if Lucille would put it together with all kinds of illustrations, graphs, pictures, and statistics, but not about people personally like in the interview when he asked you all these specific questions. The presentation would be all about how many kids were having sex, how many babies were being born to unwed mothers, how many kids got STDs, really terrible stuff, and lots of other stuff about puberty, and all that fascinating information.

But mostly it would be about what the Church taught about sex and marriage, and how sacred they were because, like Lucille says, you can't scare kids into being chaste. And it would talk all about families, and parents creating bodies for the spirits who were anxious to come to earth so they could continue progressing. All the graphics backed up with all these quotations from apostles and pictures of happy families with about ten kids having family home evening or going across the parking lot to church, everybody smiling and happy, the kids running ahead they were so happy to get to church. Yeah, sure. Give me a break.

Parents were supposed to tell their kids all this sex stuff, of course, but a lot didn't do it, and the maturation lesson in the sixth grade didn't help that much, so the three bishops set up the big sex-education night. You had to be fourteen and have your parents' written permission to go, and parents were urged to come too, which about half did, their kids sitting right next them, most of the boys looking down at the floor, the girls taking it all in, especially when it showed the new father holding the baby that had just been born. And the bishoprics and youth leaders from all three wards were there, and all the stake leaders, and the stake presidency of course, all three of them, like they were guards or something so kids wouldn't make a break for it. They probably had the outside doors locked anyway, but the refreshments helped a little.

Lucille had me helping her with the projector and audio and everything of course. President Smyles thought the presentation was so great that he asked Lucille to do it for the nine wards in the other three buildings, with a bishop doing the narrating. And of course I had to go along to help all three times.

"It'll be good for you," Lucille said when I was helping her pack her new Explorer. "It takes awhile to pound anything into that thick skull of yours."

Mark, who came once when we had it in our building, said it was all very interesting and useful information.

"Oh, just wonderful. Lucille is just full of information. If you've got any questions about sex or anything else, just get on the phone and give her a call. Maybe she'll even start a stake sex hot line."

A kid at school from our stake named Austin Fails said he felt sorry for me. I said I felt sorry for myself. So onerous.

• • •

Working in the dim light, I knocked out the bulging passenger window with the hammer. Using the jack, I pushed the window frame up so I could start clearing the snow in front of the door and force it open. I was careful the jack didn't slip. If I broke an arm or a wrist, I would be finished. Just smashing a couple of fingers would be bad. Once I got the snow cleared, I'd use the jack to get the door open.

I stopped long enough to eat. If a big spruce formed a protective roof over the Suburban, I'd be out in three or four hours anyway, at least in a day, and wouldn't even need all the food. I was still getting air, kept wondering where it was coming from. I knew there could be another slide or a big blizzard, which might stop the air, and I'd die anyway, start choking, grab my throat with both hands, just keel over. But I still kept working. You had to have faith.

I unstrapped the trenching tool and, kneeling on the passenger seat, started digging at the dirty, gray snow outside the window. Nate told me that snow in an avalanche could be hard like cement, not soft and white like you'd expect. I didn't think it would cave in on me. Digging was hard work. I threw the snow in the back of the Suburban. The main thing now was to clear the door so I could open and close it and get in and out of the Suburban. Mark and I had seen a World War II flick where the prisoners of war dug escape tunnels and put the dirt in their pockets. They had cut the ends of their pockets and tied them with string using a slip knot. Then they pulled the slip knot and let the dirt fall down their pant legs in the prison yard. Really prodigious.

I kept digging until I had enough space to stick my head and shoulders out the window and dig down so I'd have a hole to climb into and kneel. I'd started to sweat and had to take a breather and eat some more food. The paramedics said that sweating was bad because it cooled your body and could be the start of hypothermia. You had to wear long johns that absorbed the sweat.

It took me four hours to dig a hole big enough to crawl out through the window and kneel in, and another two so I could stand up, the hard, icy snow falling down onto my face. I was glad I had my ski goggles and my hat under my parka hood. I had to keep taking off the goggles to wipe them clean. The light from the Suburban was very dim inside my hole. I was saving the flashlight and the candle for the shaft. It was a big candle, maybe three inches in diameter and five long.

I kept digging down to make more space, but then I heard something very faint. I bent forward to listen. The sound seemed to come from under me. I listened. It sounded like flowing water. It had to be water. But how could there be any water?

The only water in the bowl was Crystal Creek. It ran at the far side of the bowl at the edge of the spruce-covered hill and into Silver Canyon. And then I knew where I was. The avalanche had carried the Suburban across the bowl to the creek. That's where the air was coming from, not down through the limbs of some big sheared-off spruce. The front end of the Suburban must be hanging over the creek or alongside.

I listened. Then I started digging. I uncovered a log, another log, old white logs with no limbs or bark. Nate had told me that an avalanche could shear the limbs off a big spruce or bring it down whole, not even a branch missing, and bring down big boulders too that smashed everything. I'd seen old logs like that when I fished with Grandpa Hooper.

I knocked a hole between the logs, looked down. I got the flashlight out of the glove compartment. Holding it tight with both hands, I shined it down into the hole to the dark water. My air was coming up from the creek, otherwise I would be dead. My air wouldn't get cut off. It was so worthy.

"Thank you, God, for doing that." I knew I was having faith, a little anyway.

"It's a miracle." That's what Lucille would say if she'd come with me in the Suburban. She believed in miracles, real miracles—members of the Church being saved from fires, floods, tornados, earthquakes, being warned by a voice what to do, all the miracles in the Bible and Book of Mormon. Every month the *Ensign* printed stories in the back about people who'd experienced miracles in their lives, with pictures of the moms and dads gazing up to heaven, holding their children close, tears streaming down their faces they were so grateful. Lucille used these stories in our family home evening lessons. I figured it was a miracle that I ever got through a lesson. Pretty boring. Except some of the stories were sort of interesting, sometimes.

I turned off the flashlight and stood hunched over in the dim light from the Suburban. I knew I could try dropping down into the creek and getting out that way. But I'd never make it, even if I was in great shape from lifting weights. Too many rock and log jams, the creek cutting only a narrow tunnel through the deep snow. I'd be trapped, get wet, and die from hypothermia in about an hour.

It'd taken me six hours to open the window and dig the cave. I'd never been so tired in my whole life. To reduce the chill factor, I pushed snow to block the hole I'd opened to the creek. Using the jack, I'd get the door open tomorrow. I could dig a horizontal tunnel to the end of the avalanche, but I didn't know how far it went or which way. My surest bet was to dig a shaft straight up. I'd run Grandpa Hooper's plumb line from the top so I'd always know I was going straight up and not curving off.

I took off my gloves and rubbed my hands, blew on them, and put them under my armpits, stamped my feet. The paramedics told us that in severe frostbite you could snap off fingers and toes like they were raw carrots. So lugubrious.

It would be so awesome to be able to turn on the heater, get totally warm, but even if I could start the engine, the carbon monoxide would kill me in about five minutes flat.

In Tolson's class we'd read a story about a miner in Alaska hiking to his cabin with his dog, but the miner broke through the creek ice, got his feet wet, and froze to death. It was so cold, seventy-five degrees below zero, that when he spit, the spit froze in the air and made a crackling sound. Walking out of class, I told Mark you wouldn't need a thermometer or anything to tell how cold it was. All you'd have to do was spit whenever you wanted to know.

"Oh, sure. I'm surprised you didn't ask Tolson about it. We could've had a great discussion on frozen spit."

"I thought maybe you would."

"Oh, sure. Hooper, you're so lame you ought to be in a wheelchair."

Wrapped in my quilt, I fixed my supper. The chocolate cake was kind of frozen, but it tasted so good.

I almost turned on the radio just to hear a human voice. I reached out my hand but pulled back. I knew I had to save the battery. I couldn't recharge it. I was surprised at how much self-control I was developing, which I wasn't famous for, something Lucille was always reminding me about. She was very big on self-control.

I put the flashlight back in the glove compartment. I had to be very careful. Losing or breaking it would be a catastrophe, or something worse because I'd only have the candle for light to dig by.

Wrapped up in the quilt, I looked at myself in the rearview mirror again. My face looked thin, dirty, my eyes sunken, like I was already beginning to starve to death. I reached up to touch the dried blood on the side of my head. I turned off the light, sat there in the darkness. I was still hungry. I pushed my hand against my face. I still couldn't understand how darkness could be that dark.

I said a quick prayer. Just a quick one, silent, not really closing my eyes. Lucille was always telling me to pray, to have a prayer in my heart. "You pray when you're tempted, young man. You need the guidance of the Holy Ghost most then, and don't you forget it." Oh sure. You're about to rob a liquor store, steal a car, light up a joint, turn on a porn channel, or you're on a date with some voluptuous blonde and headed to a secluded parking spot up Silver Canyon, and you suddenly start to pray for strength and be all spiritual. You'd probably get struck by lightning or the car would suddenly catch fire because of spontaneous combustion.

I knew I was going to have to dig myself out, if I could. The ski patrol wasn't going to find me. Nearly everybody would be going back to school or to work tomorrow. If I made it, I made it; if I didn't, I didn't. Grandpa always said to do your best and then accept the consequences if things don't work out. He said, "A guy who says he can't is a sucker who won't try" and "I'll lay me down to bleed awhile and I'll rise and fight again."

Falling asleep I thought about my buddies—Mark, Rob, Chris, Dave, and Jesse. They were great guys; they helped keep me in line. Mark and Chris weren't members but really great guys, especially Mark. No lily of the valley of course, but okay. Lucille said he was a fine young man and I was lucky to have him as my best friend. I knew all five of them would go over to visit Lucille and Frank because we'd all gone over to Blake Fooler's house when he drowned cliff-jumping up at Elk Reservoir. Like a dork he had to show off and jumped off a hundred-footer and drowned, without anybody knowing until after the autopsy that he'd collapsed both lungs and ruptured his spleen, so he bled to death, really done a job on himself.

Trace's friends had come to visit Frank and Lucille when Trace died. I knew that my friends would all wear suits and shirts and ties, maybe go Sunday after church, to show how much they respected me. Talking in whispers, just like when we went to Blake's place, they'd argue about who should ring the doorbell.

"You do it, Mark."

"Why don't you?"

"You were his best friend."

"Okay, okay. I don't see what difference it makes."

Mark would ring the doorbell; they'd all stand there tall and straight and looking serious. Frank would open the door because he'd be staying home because I was dead and everything was so tragic.

"Well, boys, how nice to see you." He'd turn to Lucille sitting by the fireplace, Sadie by her feet. "Honey, Kyle's friends are here. Come in, boys, please come in."

They'd all walk in and stand there in a tight group, just like at Blake's house. Frank would have to close the door behind them. Lucille would come over and stand by Frank, who'd put his arm around her shoulders.

She'd say, "Boys, it's so nice of you to come."

"We just wanted to say how sorry we are about Kyle, Mrs. Hooper." Mark would breathe in deep, like he always did when he got all uptight. "Kyle was such a really great guy."

"Please come in and sit down. Would you like a piece of chocolate cake and a glass of milk?" Lucille was always offering my friends chocolate cake and milk, like she was trying to bribe them to be good or something.

Mark would look at the others, who'd be too nervous and embarrassed to sit down. "No, thank you, Mrs. Hooper. We just wanted to say we're sorry about Kyle. He was a cool kid, really cool."

"Thank you, Mark. May I give each of you a hug?"

They'd all nod, say yes. Jess and Dave, who were a couple of wusses, would be blinking back tears. Lucille would hug them all and probably add a kiss on the cheek, too, like she always does.

"Thank you, boys. Thanks so much for coming. It's very kind of you. You're very nice boys."

"We're really sorry."

"We know you are, Chris. You boys certainly look nice."

Frank would open the front door and shake their hands and close the door behind them. They'd walk down my snow-cleared path out of the porch light.

"Why did you two have to start bawling and ruin everything?" Mark would say that.

"We weren't bawling."

"What do you call it then?"

"I don't call it anything."

"Whatever."

Third Day, Monday

Waking up, I didn't turn on the light, just sat there in the darkness wrapped in my quilt feeling all strange and scared. I'd woken up during the night, turned on the light, and eaten a couple more hot dogs and drunk a Coke. I was so hungry. Afterward, the light out, I'd thought about God. In the darkness it was easier to think about him. I'd never thought about him much or what he was like or what you did in heaven, if that's where you ended up, and not hell. In the Church we didn't really believe in hell, just the three degrees of glory, except you could end up in outer darkness, which was sort of like hell without a body, if you'd been super evil and denied Jesus and didn't even want to repent. It would be pretty awful, especially not having a body, and not being with your family and all your relatives all the way back to Adam and Eve.

Brother Glimmer told us in seminary that your personality didn't change that much when you died, so you were stuck with who you were, which is why you should keep all the commandments and try to be perfect. And finally after you'd been a spirit for a while you got your same body and everything back. And if you had an arm or a leg cut off, it was all fixed again and made perfect.

After class, Mazie Tierful said when you died you remembered all the sins you'd ever committed. And everybody else in heaven knew about them too, even your mom and dad. And then you got judged by God and had to go to the glory he sent you to, celestial, the best, terrestrial, the next best, and telestial, the worst, where I'd probably end up. There was outer darkness, where you didn't have a body but were just a spirit with the devil and tried to get people on earth to commit all these sins. But you had to be really sinful to end up there, which I didn't think I was. In heaven you always had to be progressing, becoming a better and better person all the time, whether you wanted to or not. You could never take it easy, maybe rest for a century or two and just have some fun.

I knew I didn't want to know all the sins about Lucille and Frank or Grandpa Hooper, Nate, Clay, Chase, Brooke, Jed, and Mark, or Summer, or anybody else, and didn't want them to know about me. So perfidious, and something God wouldn't do. I didn't really like to think about sin much. Mostly I just wanted to enjoy my fleeting youth. Next summer I was going to have to get a full-time job, working even on Saturday, probably twelve hours a day, and start saving most of my money for my mission the next year when I was eighteen, not be able to ever really enjoy life again.

I asked Lucille if everybody in heaven knew all about each other's sins. She said, "Who's been telling you that nonsense. God knows of course, but why should anybody else know? It would be pretty boring anyway. Nothing quite as uninteresting as sin when you think about it, in the long run anyway, because it makes you so miserable and lonely. The only interesting thing is trying to keep the commandments and seek the guidance of the Holy Ghost in your life. And use your head too of course, do your own thinking, make right decisions. You're responsible for your own life, because if you aren't I don't know who is. You'll learn that someday. At least I hope you do, for all our sakes. But mostly yours."

I didn't say anything. I didn't know what to say.

I thought it would be a lot easier just to be reincarnated

maybe, and not have to worry about keeping all the commandments and earning this big reward in heaven, if you did. We'd talked about that in the eighth grade in my world civilization class when we were discussing India. All the kids had to choose what they wanted to come back as. I decided I wanted to be a ten-foot-high-at-the-shoulders, bulletproof grizzly bear and live in Yellowstone Park and terrify all the visitors, or maybe a tiger that big, maybe a lion, maybe a condor or an eagle, maybe a great white shark, maybe a redwood tree. What would it be like to be a redwood and just stay in one place for hundreds of years, be that high? But when I really thought about it, I just wanted to be me forever and not be always dead, couldn't imagine me without my body. Really radical.

Thinking about my body, I realized again how hungry I was. It was a lot worse than fast Sunday when Lucille made me fast two whole meals, come home from fast and testimony meeting so hungry and weak I could hardly get out of the car, looking for a chance to grab about six cookies and a glass of milk so I wouldn't faint before dinner.

I turned on the dash and ceiling light and fixed my last two hot dogs, got a banana from the box, and opened a can of Coke. I liked Coke. I couldn't believe I'd eaten the whole dozen buns and wieners and all the oranges. I had the dozen hamburger buns left, but no meat, except the two pounds of frozen hamburger I'd tossed in the back of the Suburban. I'd need a Coleman stove and a frying pan to fix hamburgers, which I didn't have. I had a package of sliced cheese for cheese burgers. I'd use that with wilted lettuce, tomatoes, and sliced dill pickles. That wouldn't be so bad with mustard and catsup, as long as I had pop to wash it down. Some of the tomatoes didn't get totally smashed, so I could use them too, except they'd be sort of icy, which was okay. I'd eaten almost all of Lucille's chocolate cake. It was so good letting the thick frosting melt in my mouth, then swallowing it.

I kept thinking about Trace. The night after Trace died, I lay awake looking at his empty hospital bed and thinking about where he was in the funeral home. I could see that long stainless-steel table with the drains and that pump machine over to the side, like Willie Bodlie, whose father owned the Heavenly View Mortuary, showed Mark and me once, and I wondered if they'd started to embalm Trace yet. I tried to think it wasn't Trace but just his dead body, and that Trace was in heaven or somewhere, like a spirit or something but still with a spirit body shaped just like his old body, except different, and not just a sort of vapor or something, but still Trace. Except that didn't work, and I had to flip over and bury my head in my pillow and not think about Trace anymore. I was afraid I might start screaming because I didn't want that to ever happen to me, but I didn't scream. I'd begun to understand that as you got older there were things you didn't want to think about.

Lucille had asked me if I wanted to sleep in one of the other bedrooms that first night, like I might be scared of Trace's ghost or something, and I said no.

She said, "Well, I thought it wouldn't hurt to ask." And then she kissed me on the cheek.

All Trace's clothes were hanging in the closet and all his stuff was still on his side of the room. The hospital bed was all made, like he hadn't died there and would be back sleeping in it that night. I lay awake looking at his empty bed, wondering where he was and what he was doing, if anything.

I'd already gotten the Martin guitar Trace had given me and brought it to my side of the room. I wondered what Lucille was going to do with all his other stuff. Even a month after the funeral, Lucille kept stopping in the family room in front of the family picture board to look at shots of Trace playing tennis, playing his Martin and singing, girls sitting around looking up at him, skiing, always with some classy lovely, and all the school dances and parties, him and Laura junior prom king and queen. Lucille just stood there crying, but not loud, not even wiping off the tears, reaching up to touch the pictures, like Trace was the only one she ever really loved. I knew that wasn't true, but thinking that made me feel better when I'd done something stupid and she was hammering on me.

• • •

Sitting there in the darkness shivering, I pulled my ski hat down farther over my ears, tightened the string on my parka hood, pulled the quilt tighter around me. I was still hungry, but I knew I had to start rationing my food.

I'd done some dumb things in my life, but nothing like getting caught in the avalanche. If I'd waited for Nate, it never would have happened. Or if I hadn't stepped on my phone, I'd be all okay. I kept worrying about Lucille. Everybody telling her I was dead and she'd have to accept it whether she wanted to or not would be so tough.

Even when the doctors told her Trace was dying and Frank, President Smyles, Bishop Goodmer, and Nate, who was back from his mission, gave him blessings of comfort, she still wouldn't buy it, and kept doing everything for him, sitting on the edge of his bed holding his hand and smoothing back his hair. She kept making him all these nutritious soups, puddings, and ice cream drinks because he couldn't eat anything else.

I knew I shouldn't have given Lucille such a hard time. She had a whole list of dumb things Mark and I and the other guys had done that she dragged out to remind me of when necessary, like the Tolson white mice incident, which is what she called it, and like skinny-dipping in the Millwells' swimming pool at two in the morning and getting caught and old man Millwell grabbing our clothes and calling our folks and making us stay in the pool until they got there, or setting the weeds in the vacant lot on fire so the fire department came roaring up, or turning Dallin Cherry's druggie brother's eight-foot-long python loose in the girls' locker room at school, or drinking half a twelve-pack of beer Mark and I bought from some kid for five dollars and getting drunk, which Lucille found out about later somehow, or finding half a case of dynamite, a coil of fuse, and dynamite caps in an abandoned prospect in Silver Canyon and spending the whole day blowing up rocks, trees, and old mine shacks, until Sheriff Catchwell nailed our butts.

But then Nate had wrecked two of Frank's cars, and Clay set fire to an old barn when he and his friends were lying around on a big pile of straw smoking pot. So Lucille drove old Nate to school every day for two weeks, sat in all of his classes and labs, ate lunch with him, waited for him outside the restroom, told him she'd come in with him if necessary, till he pleaded with her to stop.

"Please, Mom, I'll never smoke pot again. I'll go on a mission. I'll get straight A's. Just please don't come to school with me anymore. Please, Mom. It's so embarrassing. I can't stand it. I'm a senior."

"Well, we'll see. Let's just finish out the week. It's only Tuesday."

"Mom, please."

"We'll talk about it tonight after you've got all your homework done."

Of course, old Trace never seemed to do anything really dumb. The perfect son, which Lucille never failed to mention on occasion. "Why can't you be more like Trace?"

"Because I don't want to be." Which of course I didn't say. I was smarter than that. I may not have been perfect, but I wasn't exactly involved in any actual felonious activities either, at least as far as I could tell. You had to be sort of careful that way, a little.

Lucille would close her eyes and shake her head. "I don't know whether I'm going to survive your adolescence or not,

Kyle. I survived your brothers', but I'm not sure about you. Do you think you and Mark and the rest of those friends of yours will ever grow up, begin to think a little bit about consequences?"

"We just wanted to have a little fun. Nobody got hurt."

"Just having fun? Well, you and I and Mark and his poor overworked mother have all got an appointment with Principal Jagger in the morning at nine about that minor incident you two were involved in last Friday, climbing out the classroom window and walking along a thirty-foot-high ledge to escape class. We'll see how much fun that's going to be. I'm not so sure about Mark, who on occasion seems to show some sense, but what you seem to want is juvenile delinquency."

"Ah, Mom."

"Don't you 'Ah, Mom' me, young man."

I warned Mark about Lucille. "Look," I said, "you join the Mormon church and you have to pay tithing, that's ten percent of everything you earn, and start saving your own money to pay for a mission the Church sends you on when you're just eighteen. You can't go skiing or do anything fun on Sunday. On Saturday you have all these service projects cleaning up old widows' yards, and you have to promise to earn your Eagle. They make you a deacon when you're only twelve, and you have to go out and collect fast offerings, pass the sacrament, and then they make you a teacher when you're fourteen, and you prepare the sacrament, and still have to do all the things the deacons do, and then a priest when you're sixteen, so you have to bless it and still do everything else too. They make you an elder just to send you on a mission for two years when you just graduated from high school the week before, are only eighteen, and might have time for some real fun finally, and so you have to be super righteous and spiritual. You can't date or even kiss a girl while you're gone or they excommunicate you. And then when you come home you have to get married within six months and start having about ten kids to provide all these bodies for waiting spirits. You're broke, work part time, go to school full time too, have to borrow about a hundred thousand dollars to pay tuition, which you'll spend your whole life paying back. And have to live in this dinky basement apartment and buy all your clothes at Deseret Industries. And your folks invite you to dinner every Sunday and send you home with all the leftovers so your pregnant wife won't starve during the week. And when you do finally graduate, they make you an elders quorum president, then a bishop, and a stake president, and you never ever have any free time because you're a doctor or a bank president or something. You don't know what you're getting into."

"Look, I'm not joining your church. But I like blessing the food, family prayer, and family home evening and the lessons. I just like it. Your mom's a great cook. She makes these great pies, cookies, and cakes. Besides, my mom says I need all the religion I can get."

"Well, just remember, I warned you. Lucille's on your trail."

• • •

Leaning forward in the seat, I checked the dash clock. I knew I had to get to work digging the shaft, but I was so cold. I pulled the quilt up around my head, tightened down into it, kept thinking about Lucille and what she was doing and all the things she'd tried to teach me and wanted me to do, especially because of my birthday, hitting me with that.

"You're going to be sixteen soon and your father's going to ordain you a priest, and you'll be up in front of the whole ward blessing the sacrament. You need to think about what that means."

I did think about it. Breaking the bread, kneeling to say the prayer, Frank at the sacrament table to say one of the prayers with me because that was the tradition in the Mountain View Ward your first time as a new priest. And then looking over at Bishop Goodmer seeing if you did it right, and him giving you the nod, or shaking his head and you had to do it over. And when you sat at the sacrament table just before the meeting, you worried Bishop Goodmer might stand up and come over and say perhaps you shouldn't bless the sacrament today, Kyle, or maybe he'd say Brother Hooper just to be nice, but he meant you, not your dad, and you had to leave the sacrament table. And everybody would know you were guilty of some big unrepented sin or something, which you were, Frank just sitting there looking at you, and Lucille and the rest of the family because it was your first time blessing the sacrament. And Bishop Goodmer would be all inspired or something so he would know what you'd done, even though you hadn't confessed. And he'd tell you to meet him in his office after the meeting to straighten things out because you weren't righteous enough yet. So ominous.

But if that didn't happen, you got to bless the bread or the water, reading the prayer, thinking about what the words meant about Jesus' flesh and blood, suffering for everybody in the whole world who'd ever lived, words you'd heard every Sunday of your life, pretty serious words. Now you were saying them for the whole ward, your dad right there beside you, Lucille so thrilled she was probably crying because you were actually worthy to bless the sacrament finally. So you really had to think about the words, your heart pounding, hands sweating, trying to keep your voice steady. Because for the first time in your life you really understood they were important, kneeling there feeling the Spirit just a little maybe, for the first time in your life, sort of worthy.

• • •

I checked the dash clock again. The light was so dim. It made me feel sad. Ten o'clock Monday morning. I really needed to get to sleep for at least a week. I kept looking at the clock. I should have been sitting in Miss Tolson's English class. I could hear Tolson saying what a terrible tragedy it was I was killed in the avalanche, because Jagger had made the intercom announcement first period, and everybody would know I was dead after two whole days. Tolson would stand looking at the class, probably smiling, trying to be cheerful.

I didn't like to think of people saying I'd been killed, because I hadn't been killed yet. I could just hear old Tolson standing there in front of the class.

"Kyle was such a wonderful young man. He was always kind and thoughtful, and always had a smile on his face. He was a student with wonderful potential. He loved to study great literature. We will all miss him so much. But then life is full of tragedy, as we all know who have studied Shakespeare and the other great writers. We must learn to endure tragedy. It is what helps to make us all human. As we know, this is one of the purposes of all great literature."

Tolson would probably whip out some tragic poem to read, probably the to-be-or-not-to-be soliloquy from old *Hamlet*. We'd all had to memorize it, guys from class saying, "To be or not to be; that is the question," when they saw you in the halls, or walking up to some voluptuous girl and whispering it in her ear. Tolson would probably have the whole class recite it in unison because of me. And then the grief counselor would come in, and they would have to go through that farce.

It always surprised me how much girls like to cry. I guessed it made them feel better. You'd see two girls talking in the hall, and one would be crying telling the other one something, probably about some football player who'd dumped her the night before, the other girl hugging her because it was so terribly tragic. And then an hour later you'd see that same girl talking to some other guy, probably another football player, and smiling, like women could turn it off and on like a faucet. Makes you wonder. It all seems so inconsequential when you really think about it, but helps make girls kind of strange and interesting, mysterious, and you know you're going to be spending the rest of your life trying to figure them out, especially your wife.

Laura, a really classy blonde with lips worth marrying for, came to be with Trace every day after school when he got sick. And Lucille told me not to go into my own bedroom while Laura was there. One afternoon walking down the hall I saw Laura sitting on Trace's bed holding both his hands in both of hers. And then she reached up with one hand to smooth back his long curly hair that all the girls thought was so wonderful, and then Laura kissed Trace on the lips. He didn't have to do anything; she just kissed him. So worthy. I couldn't believe old perfect Trace had ever kissed a girl, even once.

Lucille had straightened me out on too much kissing and making out, which could lead to *promiscuity*, another word I didn't like the sound of.

I'd made the mistake once of telling Lucille that a girl at school named Annie Wail had gotten pregnant. "But she's nothing but a slut, a whore really, must weigh a ton. All the boys at school know that."

"A slut, a whore? What do you call the boy that got her pregnant, a whoremonger? Probably not, you boys don't even know what the word means. But that's what he is. You might mention that to Jefferson High's male population, have them look it up in the dictionary. The poor hapless Annie. She's fifty pounds overweight and wants to be popular so bad that she was willing to do almost anything. Or she thought she'd fallen in love and somehow nothing mattered but that, so she gave Sir Galahad what he wanted most in life because he loved her so much he just couldn't stand it and didn't have the brains or the time to use a condom. So she's pregnant, the poor kid, totally miserable, and Galahad probably doesn't even remember her name the next day. She drops out of school, has the baby, and if she isn't smart enough to give it up for adoption, which she probably isn't because she loves it so much, her parents get to raise it, because in three or four months Annie's decided she wants her life back, whatever there is to get back, and walks out."

"Ah, Mom, she's not the only one."

"Of course not. How could she be with all those horny boys wandering around loose? And don't you ever let me hear you call a girl a slut or a whore again. I hoped you had at least that much charity in you or, barring that, at least some sense."

"Ah, Mom."

"Don't you 'Ah, Mom' me."

• • •

I looked at the windshield, the inside frost thicker. I was surprised there weren't icicles. I thought about the heater again. I'd heard that carbon monoxide was an easy way to die. Freezing to death was an easy way too. The paramedics told us about that; you just went to sleep. But starving to death wasn't easy. Everybody knew that. You just got weaker and weaker until you couldn't even move. I'd seen pictures of people in concentration camps in World War II who were starving, their bones sticking through, the skin tight around their skulls so that their staring eyes were bigger, and stacks of dead people all around. But I figured I'd probably die of hypothermia or even freeze before I'd starve to death. I'd heard of missionaries fasting and praying for days so their investigators would get a testimony and join the Church, so starving was sort of like that, I guess, only worse of course and took longer.

Pushing back the quilt, I rubbed my cold hands. I took off

my ski boots and rubbed my feet. In this documentary I saw where this mountain climber phoned his wife to say goodbye because he was trapped and dying, all the other climbers got frostbitten fingers and toes, which turned black. If the frostbite was severe enough, the team doctor had to cut them off. Your ears and nose could get frostbitten too and have to be cut off. That would be so terrible. I didn't want anything cut off, I knew that. I decided that mountain climbers must have special insulated face masks, and hoods and jackets, and long johns and pants for protection.

I closed my eyes: "Please, God, please help me to get back home so Lucille won't be so sad. Please. And please send the Holy Ghost to help teach me what to do. In the name of Jesus, amen." It seemed important to say that, like I was really serious or something and knew I was responsible.

The keys were still in the ignition, the ignition turned off. I must have done that. I guess it was just instinct. It was a good thing, or the battery would be dead. Tim Mashly rolled his dad's new Ford pickup five times off a switchback and back down on the road up Bear Canyon. The top was all crushed in except for a bubble over the driver, and the windows and windshield were busted out. It lit on all four wheels. Nobody saw Tim roll. And when Tim turned the key, the engine started, so the battery wasn't hurt. He drove the Ford home at three in the morning, parked in his driveway, and went to bed without telling his dad because he was so tired and had had such a tough time. When his dad went to work early and saw his new smashed pickup, he went in and dragged Tim out of bed, shouting at him all the way down the hall, dragged him outside just in his shorts and T-shirt, stood him there on the porch shouting at him.

"Look at that new pickup! Just look at it! My beautiful brand-new red Ford pickup! You blockhead!"

And then Tim said his mom came out to see what all the

shouting was about and said, "You should be grateful your son wasn't killed."

"Grateful? Grateful?"

"Yes, grateful. Of course, grateful."

Tim said his dad looked at his mom. "Grateful? I'm supposed to be grateful? That numbskull son of yours wrecks my new red Ford pickup, and I'm supposed to be grateful?" Turning, cussing all the way, his dad got in his car and went to work.

"It was so awesome, Kyle," Tim told me, "I didn't know my dad could cuss like that. He goes to church every Sunday."

I looked down at the keys. I reached out from the quilt and touched them. I couldn't help myself. I had to know if the motor would start, like Tim's dad's Ford pickup. I put my foot on the gas. I turned the key. The engine caught. I turned it off. It thrilled me to hear the engine. So commodious. I'd glanced at the gas gauge. About six gallons. If I could run the engine, I could get warm and charge the battery. I'd have a light for hours, even run the radio. It would be so great to hear human voices again.

"All you need, Kyle baby, is a long hose to attach to the exhaust pipe and run down into Crystal Creek or somewhere so you don't die of carbon monoxide poisoning. And then of course you'd have to cut a tunnel around to the back of the Suburban to attach it. But you haven't got a hose. Too bad. Of course, the muffler and the exhaust pipe could be punctured or broken, which they probably are, so a hose wouldn't work anyway, would it?"

Grandpa Hooper fixed all his own cars. When he worked on one in his garage and had to run the engine, he attached a long hose to the exhaust to get rid of the carbon monoxide. Taking the sucker out of his mouth, he always warned me about getting asphyxiated. I wished the hose was in the Suburban. It had hung on the wall in the garage when Frank sold the house.

I knew I had to get to work digging myself out. I pushed back the quilt. Lying on the front seat face down, I braced the jack against the seat legs and the door. It kept slipping, and it took me an hour to force the front passenger door open wide enough that I could get out into the hole I'd dug and didn't have to climb through the window anymore.

I stopped to eat. I finished off the last of the chocolate cake. I couldn't help myself.

Working in the dim light from the Suburban, I opened up the hole between the two logs above Crystal Creek so I could dump the snow from my shaft. I had to keep stopping to take off my gloves and blow on my fingers. The icy snow fell into my face, fogging my goggles.

The overhead light coming through the open door helped, but I would need the flashlight when I got higher. I could dig a tunnel to the front fender and use the parking light, but it was too far away from my shaft. The headlights wouldn't work either and would pull too much power anyway. I knew I had to keep thinking, having faith, and praying.

I cut the shaft about two feet in diameter. I thought I might break through to the surface any minute because the avalanche might not be so deep at the end. If my head suddenly just popped up out of the snow and I started yelling, the ski patrol would all go nuts. That'd be so awesome. I dug faster.

I stopped for lunch. I took off my gloves, licked the end of my finger to pick up all the crumbs in the cake pan.

I kept thinking about those great Sunday dinners Lucille always cooked, with Nate, Clay, and Brooke and Jed, and Trace before he died usually there, and Frank too some of the time—roast, or maybe chicken, mashed potatoes, gravy, about three kinds of vegetables, hot rolls, salad, Lucille's special fruit punch, and then dessert, usually her special pie or chocolate cake with ice cream. Everybody sitting around the table talking and laughing, and telling what they'd been doing that week. And then in the evening before everybody left and we had family prayer, another serving of dessert, all of us sitting around the fire in the family room. Lucille always asked me if Mark's mother was working on Sunday; if she was, Lucille told me to be sure and invite him for supper. I knew what she was up to, but it was okay. Mark never said no. He liked my whole family. He told me how lucky I was.

"Oh sure," I said, "except when Lucille has me on her radar. You ought to try that sometime."

"You're still lucky."

"I guess."

• • •

At first I worked in the light from the Suburban, but then I had to use the flashlight. I cut a hole in the side of the shaft to put it in, very careful not to drop it. After the flashlight was finished, all I had was my candle.

"It can't be any deeper than twenty, it just can't be. Please, God, don't let it be any deeper than that, please. I'll do anything for you when I get out. I'll go to church every Sunday. I won't ever swear again, tell any lies, or cheat on tests, and even stop thinking about girls till I'm twenty and back from my mission. I'll finish earning my Eagle. I'll go on two missions. God, please, I'll stop swearing right now. In the name of Jesus, amen."

I kept saying that to myself. But I knew that God didn't work that way. At least I didn't think he did. He didn't have to make bargains; he was God. Besides, I knew I probably couldn't keep the bargains anyway, or I'd forget. Lucille was always telling me I was very forgetful when it came to keeping promises about changing my behavior, and I guess I was.

I knew Lucille would be praying for me. Dr. Wellmen told her three times Trace wasn't going to make it, so in the family prayers when Trace was in a coma she prayed he would have faith and believe in Jesus and the resurrection and that we'd all be together as a family again, and there would be Grandma and Grandpa Hooper to be with him till we all died. I hoped Frank was still home to help Lucille out. He'd only stayed home three full days when Trace died.

• • •

The hardened snow came off in chunks sometimes, but mostly in pieces like shaved ice, spraying down into my face. I ran into rocks and small broken spruce limbs that were hard to dig out or cut up. Even if a ninety-foot spruce probably was keeping the Suburban from being crushed, I sure didn't want to have to cut through any limbs a foot or two thick with my bow saw. Maybe I could just tunnel around them if I had to.

I'd cut two feet up into the shaft from the top of the cave when I quit. Tomorrow I'd have to start cutting footholds. If I didn't run into any big spruce limbs or boulders, I could cut four or five feet a day, at least. I was going to get out. I knew it. I just had to keep working. I almost wanted to cry I was so happy.

I kept thinking about it being Christmas, the house full of the smell of good things to eat, with plates of homemade cookies and candy and hot spiced cider so you could have as much as you wanted. There'd be stacks of presents under the tree, and you'd already checked out how many had your name on them. The whole family would be home Christmas Eve, and they'd sit by the fire drinking Lucille's hot chocolate and eating her homemade donuts, Sadie lying down by me because she was really my dog. I'd go to all the Christmas parties with Mark, and we'd kiss girls under the mistletoe, or just kiss them because it was Christmas. Girls liked to be kissed at Christmas, like they were being extra generous or something, every kiss some kind of little present, which was all right with me and Mark, the more Christmas spirit the better. I'd already made a deal with Mark that this spring when I was sixteen and there was a full moon, because girls think that's important, he was going to drive me around to all these girls' houses we knew. And I'd ring the doorbell and they'd come out on the porch, and I'd see how many girls I could kiss in one night

"About one," Mark said, "if you're lucky. You haven't got the moves, Hooper."

"I've been practicing."

"Practicing? What, in front of a mirror? Hooper, you can't practice something like that. It takes real experience."

"I'll get experience. I might just be more of a voluptuary than you think."

"A what? There you go again."

"It means you kind of like to enjoy yourself."

"Why don't you just say that then?"

"It doesn't sound as interesting."

"Doesn't sound as interesting. Hooper, just give me a break."

· · ·

Standing by the open Suburban door after I got down from the shaft, I leaned forward and held the flashlight on the dash clock. Nine-ten at night.

I'd lost track of time. It didn't matter. It was as if the whole world had suddenly gone dark. It made me feel heavy and slow and sad. Light was so important.

I was so beat and tired I could hardly move, my stomach empty and tight, the feeling coming up into my chest.

Turning, I thought I saw something move at the edge of the hole I'd opened up to push the ice and snow down through the logs to Crystal Creek.

I waited, kept the flashlight on the logs. Must have been my imagination. Then a mink poked its black head up between the logs. I watched. So worthy. I wanted him to climb up on the log so I could see all of him, but he vanished. I turned off the flashlight and then turned it on again. But he didn't come back.

It thrilled me to see the mink and know something else was alive under the avalanche and could go up and down Crystal Creek. If I was with Grandpa fishing and we saw a mink, he always threw it the smallest fish in his basket.

I ate four more hamburger-bun sandwiches, another banana, and drank two cans of Pepsi for supper. I knew I shouldn't eat so much, but I couldn't stop myself. I wanted to open the pork and beans and eat the whole can, but I knew I had to really start rationing my food. I'd decided I really didn't know how long it would take me to dig out, maybe one or two more days. I had to keep up my strength.

Taking off my boots and gloves, I checked to see if my toes and fingers were turning white, which the paramedics said was the first sign of frostbite. They still looked a little pinkish if I rubbed long enough. The frost inside the suburban was thicker; I expected to see icicles hanging down pretty soon.

I wrapped in the quilt and turned off the light. I thought about my family and what they would be doing. On a regular Monday night if I wasn't dead and they weren't all so sad, everybody would come for family home evening. After the lesson, which Lucille always taught, even if Frank was home, we'd have kneeling prayer. And then Lucille would bring out one of her desserts—apple pie, chocolate cake, jelly roll, or cookies and homemade ice cream, or something. We'd sit around the lit fireplace in the family room talking, especially if Nate and Clay and Brooke and Jed were all there, just like on Sunday. It was so great, but it was sad at first after Trace died. Whoever said the family prayer had to remember him and say how much we loved and missed him and hoped he was enjoying himself in heaven and progressing and we'd all be together again someday.

One Monday at school I'd told Mark all about family home evening, and he'd wanted to know what it was all about. And then I'd made the mistake of telling Lucille. And so of course she'd told me to invite Mark, although I'd warned him he would have to listen to a lesson. Mark liked Lucille's desserts. His mom didn't cook much because she ran the business office for this big restaurant chain and had to work late and on weekends a lot, so he didn't get many cooked dinners with desserts.

Mark and the other guys liked to come to my house to study if Tolson was giving one of her big tests. Lucille always checked on us to see we did the homework before we started goofing off. We had a big open basement family room with a ping-pong table, pool table, stereo, wide-screen TV, and PlayStation 2.

Lucille always brought us down a big bowl of buttered popcorn, cookies and milk, cake, or ice cream or something.

"I thought you boys would be faint with hunger after all that studying." I could just hear her saying that, and the guys saying, "Oh, thank you, Mrs. Hooper. Thank you, thank you."

"Thanks, Mom."

"Your mom is so great."

"Yeah, I know."

I actually didn't mind writing papers for old Tolson's class, especially if they were about some novel we'd read or about ourselves, which Tolson said was exploring our personalities, learning who we really were. I liked writing that kind of paper the best. I usually got at least a B+, which of course I always brought home and showed to Lucille, who would always say, "Oh, we know you've got brains, Kyle. Now let's start doing A work in algebra, chemistry, physics, and a few other classes."

"Oh, sure, Mom."

I really had such an easy, comfortable life. When I got out of the avalanche, I was going to be grateful for everything from now on. I was going to thank people when they did things for me, do what Frank and Lucille told me, and think about what I was doing more.

As soon as I got my license so I could legally drive, I was going to start dating up a storm, not just hang out. I'd really wanted to date earlier of course, but without a car that would have been pretty lame. It was going to be so great to go on a big date every weekend and drive up to the girl's house, ring the doorbell, and have her dad come to the door, so I had to introduce myself and have him give me the once over because he didn't want his baby girl going out with some troll. And then wait for the lovely to come down the winding stairs and into the room all beautiful, smiling, fragrant, wearing this dress all silky red, and know it was all because she liked me. I knew Summer liked me. At school if she couldn't stop in the hall and talk because she had a class or something, she always smiled and said hi and gave me a little wave. It would be great to have her as my girlfriend.

Mark and I talked a lot about these different girls we knew at school. He came over almost every night, ate supper with us about half the time. Mark had one sister, but she was married and lived in California. I knew Lucille was just softening him up. Of course, he had to have prayer and scriptures with us if he made a mistake and stayed too late. Lucille would even send home a baggie full of cookies for a snack before he went to bed or a slice of cake or pie on a paper plate, and she was always talking about the Church. I kept trying to warn Mark, but it didn't do any good. He said it was interesting talking to Lucille.

"I like to talk about religion. Your mom really knows a lot. A prophet started your church, and he translated the Book of Mormon from gold plates and everything. And a prophet is the head of your church today. And you believe people get resurrected with real bodies, and that you're in your family after you die and everything, so I could see my dad again and be with him. So really awesome."

"Yeah, well, don't ever say I didn't warn you."

Mark even started coming to seminary, not every morning but two or three times a week, old Brother Glimmer full of smiles, greeting him at the door, shaking his hand, like one of those lost sheep had just wandered in somehow. I couldn't believe Mark would sacrifice a whole hour's sleep just for seminary.

"I suppose seminary's interesting too."

"Very interesting. You're lucky."

"I know how lucky I am. I have to give up an hour's sleep every morning for four long years."

Of course, Lucille gave me that old routine about being a good example for Mark so he'd want to be like me and join the Church.

"It's very important, Kyle."

"Oh, sure. Nothing more fun than being a good example."

Nephi in the Book of Mormon got on my nerves. He was such a good example, always giving Laman and Lemuel a hard time. It would have been encouraging if old Nephi had pulled a fast one once in a while and then been forgiven or something. Corianton took off after some harlot named Isabel while he was on his mission, which was really bad, and not something a missionary should do, of course. But Alma his father, who was a prophet and everything, didn't excommunicate him or anything. He let old Corianton go back into the mission field, after he read him the riot act of course, which took about five chapters. *Harlot* was sort of an interesting word, sounded all biblical, kind of professional, and tough. I wondered if there were any harlots wandering around Silver City. I was going to ask Lucille, but then decided not to. I didn't want to get her started on that one. Of course, the sons of Helaman weren't so bad, fighting and getting wounded and bleeding all over the place till they fainted. Guys like me, teenagers, really heroic; they must have had girlfriends who visited them in the hospital, admired all those wounds all bandaged up, told them how brave they were. They'd take them good things to eat, although probably not brownies, but bananas, grapes, and coconuts, stuff like that out of the jungle.

• • •

It was so dark in the Suburban. Shivering, totally beat, wanting to fall asleep so badly, but still hungry, I said, "Just keep helping me please, God, Jesus, and Grandpa Hooper, and the Holy Ghost too. Please." I didn't say amen. It wasn't a prayer, just a request. I knew I needed help. I didn't know who else to ask.

I kept thinking about walking in the house and hollering, "Hey, Mom!" just like I did every day when I got home from school. It was going to be so great. All I had to do was keep digging the shaft and I'd make it. I'd cut a scratch on the dashboard for the three days I'd been buried, just like in the flicks where prisoners did that on the sides of their cells with chalk or a piece of rock. They cut six marks down and one across for each week, the cell walls covered with hundreds of weeks because they'd been prisoners for about twenty years.

I kept worrying about another avalanche or big snow storm so I'd never dig out. But I didn't believe God would do that to me. I was a pretty good kid, I thought, all things considered, which even Lucille admitted when she was feeling particularly magnanimous, which wasn't every day of course.

Fourth Day, Tuesday

All night I woke up every hour because I was cold. My hands and feet were numb again, especially my feet. Under the quilt I rubbed my hands hard. Maybe I'd wake up one morning and my feet and hands would be frozen. What would I do then? Mountain climbers sometimes had to beat their hands against their bodies to get the blood circulating again every morning. I could die of hypothermia during the night, wake up dead and not even know it. Or I'd wake up and be dying, knowing all the time that's what I was doing, not even able to move my arms or legs, my eyes open like I was watching myself die. It had happened. I'd read about a mountain climber who woke up in the tent, and his buddy in a sleeping bag lying right next to him didn't move but had his eyes open. The climber kept shouting at him, but he was dead, with his eyes wide open, like he was watching himself die. And the climber had to turn on the tent heater and thaw him out before he could close his eyes.

"No." I said that to myself.

I didn't shout. I said it quietly, almost like a whisper. I pushed back the quilt and turned on the light. I took off my gloves, which I wore all night, and looked at my fingers; they weren't black, but red and wrinkled. I rubbed my hands together hard. I took off my boots and rubbed my feet until they felt warm. I looked to see if any icicles had formed during the night from my breath.

I looked around. Everything was so dim. It was like the dimness was in me too. I wanted everything to be bright and full of light.

For breakfast I ate three more hamburger-bun sandwiches and a smashed banana. I drank two cans of Pepsi to make me feel full. I was starting to run out of food. I picked up a potato chip from off the passenger seat and ate that. I picked up all the other potato chips that weren't smashed because I'd stepped on them or they'd wilted from the snow. I knew I wasn't really starving, at least not yet. I looked at my thin face in the rearview mirror. I felt my arms.

I knew I had to get to work digging myself out. I couldn't just sit there. Unwrapping the quilt, I got the flashlight out of the glove compartment.

Standing in the cave, the lit flashlight in the hole, I used the trenching tool like a big chisel, kept stabbing up, the ice and snow falling into my face. I had to be careful not to crack myself on the head or get hit with rock that broke loose. I dropped the rocks and pieces of sawed off spruce branches to the bottom of the shaft.

I couldn't stop thinking about food. Lucille wouldn't let me out of the house unless I had a good breakfast.

"At least I'll know you aren't living exclusively on pop and candy bars." Lucille wasn't one of these super-righteous Mormons who wouldn't drink a Coke because it had caffeine in it, just like coffee. She said there was nothing in the Word of Wisdom about caffeine, as far as she knew. She said all pop was bad for you because of all the sugar, so it didn't make that much difference which kind.

She always asked me if I had money for lunch. She kept money in a box on top of the fridge for me so I could always grab a couple of bucks if I needed it. I always had to kiss her goodbye before I could get out of the house. She'd smooth the hair back out of my eyes and remind me again that I needed a haircut, but Lucille didn't push me on it. Girls liked my hair long. They liked to reach up and touch it. So worthy. If Mark came by early Lucille would always ask him what he'd had for breakfast. If it was only a bowl of Wheaties or something because his mom had to leave for work early, Lucille made him sit down and eat. And of course he had to pray with us and listen to Lucille read the morning scripture so we'd be inspired all day. So breakfast wasn't really free. Driving to school, Mark kept telling me what a great mom I had.

"Oh, just delightful."

Lucille wouldn't even let me have a computer in my bedroom. I had to use the one in the family room just off the kitchen because she thought I might start watching porn or play video games all night. And I'd tell her that she didn't really trust me, and she said no, she didn't. I'd say that really sucked, and she'd give me this line about Brooke, Nate, Clay, and Trace not having computers in their bedrooms and they managed to survive their raging hormones, and that sex wasn't the most important thing in life, although that probably came as a surprise to me, and that she hoped I wasn't too disappointed.

"I'm not disappointed."

"You're not? Good. Will wonders never cease. You're making some progress anyway. Don't forget to take money for your lunch. Wouldn't want you starving and too weak to go to the school dance tonight."

"Mom, why do you always say that about wonders?"

"Do I? Well, it's true isn't it?"

"Oh, sure."

The first week of class in September I had noticed some new kid in world history right across from me in the next row watching something on his laptop. The kid bent forward, using both arms to hide it, but I could still see it was porn, all these naked bodies. It was so gross. I wanted to throw my history book at him. Really gross. I didn't know the kid's name.

I watched him when the bell rang and he stood up. He kept blinking his eyes. I saw him later in the cafeteria off in a corner alone looking at it again. So pathetic.

Lucille had straightened me out on porn when I was nine.

"It's not just the pornography, Kyle. But for a teenage boy it usually involves masturbation." Which she'd also straightened me out on when I was about nine or ten. "It's a phase nearly all boys go through, but it doesn't have to become a hobby. Wet dreams are much more interesting and maturing for a boy." And then she explained all about that particular phenomenon and, just like Bishop Goodmer would about five years later, said that masturbation was serious if it became compulsive or a boy became overwhelmed with guilt because he'd always thought he was perfect and would probably maybe become an apostle or something."Don't look so embarrassed, Kyle. Biological facts are still facts, after all."

"Yeah, sure, Mom. Thanks a lot."

When I told Mark what Lucille had told me, Mark said I was lucky.

"What do you mean lucky? It's embarrassing to have your mom tell you stuff like that. It's bad enough if your dad tells you."

"Just lucky, that's all. Your mom tells you things you need to know. You got a sister and brothers, and your dad's alive. Your mom works part time at the hospital, but not because she has to. Your family gets together all the time for suppers and parties and everything. You have a cabin, and your Grandpa Hooper was so great and taught you to build things and fish and ski. You have two family reunions every summer, with all your cousins and uncles and aunts and grandpa and grandma, and all that good food. And you go to church where everybody is so friendly and you have all kinds of activities, including high adventure with the varsity Scouts. And your mom tells you all this stuff ,and she's such a great cook. I wish my mom was a nurse, and my dad was alive, and I had a big family like that. It'd be so great to have brothers. You're just lucky."

"I'll think about it."

"You really are, Kyle."

"Okay, okay. You know who you sound like, don't you?"

"Who?"

"Three guesses."

"You're always saying that."

"Only because it's true."

• • •

I had to keep stopping to warm my hands. I was so cold, tired, and hungry. I knew I was slowing down, the hypothermia starting to take over. If I ran into a long spruce limb a foot thick, I knew I'd be in trouble. It would take hours to cut through it on both sides with the bow saw, either that or dig around it. I wished Mark was there to spell me and to talk to, but I didn't want Mark to maybe die too, which I knew was possible.

I knew I was working as hard as I could to dig myself out, but I just wanted to be warm, turn on the heater, sit there and just be warm all the time, and not have to move.

I kept thinking about writing a note, in case I didn't make it, and what I would say. They'd find the note on the seat by my body. Everybody would be so sorry because it would be so tragic, especially Lucille, who'd wish she hadn't been so tough on me. And they would print the note in the *Silver City Herald* and maybe show it on TV news. And I'd have an obituary in the *Herald* just like my Grandpa Hooper and Trace and the guys from school who OD'd or killed themselves in rollovers and head-ons, or committed suicide, which they never said in the obituary, but just that he died, but not of natural causes, which they nearly always said. Like what actually killed them was some big terrible, mysterious disease like the plague or something they didn't want people to know about, and you wanted to know what natural causes were like.

I'd read Trace's obituary twice, looked at his picture, read all of his accomplishments—straight-A student, captain of the varsity tennis team, Eagle Scout, guitarist, singer, president of his seminary class. I knew that my own list of accomplishments wouldn't be very long. I was only a Second Class Scout, but I didn't think my family would put that in. All three of my brothers had earned their Eagles. Maybe they'd say I was on the track team and a boy with a lot of potential. Lucille was always talking about how smart I was and my potential, if I'd ever get around to settling down and applying myself.

Trace's funeral had lasted almost two hours. He'd had five speakers, including Principal Jagger, his Venturer leader, his physics teacher, and Mr. Boreman, who ran student government. They all said what an outstanding student and wonderful young man Trace was, what a tragedy his early death was and how he'd be missed. Brother Faither, his seminary teacher, said that he was so spiritual and had such a strong testimony that he was needed on the other side to do missionary work with the spirits in prison. I couldn't believe it. I wanted to stand up and say, "Sure, tell Trace that." The whole Jefferson High a cappella choir came and sang three songs. If Trace had come home once just slightly drunk, or even just with the smell of beer on his breath, it would have made my life a lot easier.

Standing in the receiving line with the rest of the family during the viewing before the funeral, I kept looking over at Trace in the open casket, but it didn't look like Trace. I kept saying to myself, "That's my brother Trace." But I didn't believe it. People I didn't even know kept shaking my hand and telling me how sorry they were, the women hugging Lucille, some of them crying, the men shaking my dad's hand and patting me on the shoulder, telling me what a wonderful brother Trace had been and they knew how much I was going to miss him. A lot of girls from Trace's junior class came through, all teary-eyed, looking down at Trace, holding each other's hands. They shook my hand, smiled. I thought Trace's girlfriend Laura, her lips all shiny, might give me a little hug, so warm and soft, because she knew me, and I was Trace's little brother who needed to be comforted, but she didn't.

Sitting with my family at the front of the chapel during the funeral, I kept looking at Trace's casket with the big floral wreath on top and thinking that Trace was inside and he was dead. After the prayer at the end of the viewing, the mortician had screwed down the casket lid and locked it. I wanted to ask him why, and if he thought Trace was going to sit up and shake hands with everybody one last time.

Lucille set me straight about Trace being perfect. A couple of weeks after the funeral, I'd pulled some fast one and she was reading me the riot act, and she said, "And one other thing, I want you know that Trace wasn't perfect, in spite of what they said at the funeral. He was a wonderful young man, but he wasn't perfect. Nobody's perfect in this life."

"Well, that's a relief."

"A relief? What do you mean, relief? You just work on keeping the commandments and sensing the Holy Ghost in your life. That's what spiritual means. Perfection isn't something you have to worry very much about, I don't think."

"Oh, I don't."

Lucille didn't say anything. Silent, she just looked at me and shook her head, like she was filled with despair, or something worse.

Lucille was always telling me about the Holy Ghost. He was supposed to guide you and direct you, warn you about danger, teach you all this stuff, and help you keep the commandments. Which was okay by me. I told Lucille that in a seminary testimony meeting a girl named Mary Simply said all she had to do was turn her life over to the Holy Ghost, just feel him directing everything she did, telling her what to do every minute of her life, like she was on some celestial guidance system or something. Lucille sure set me straight on that one.

"That's nonsense, absolute nonsense. You start just following your feelings and you'll be in jail in twenty-four hours. The commandments are there to be obeyed, help you decide right and wrong. You have to think about things, make decisions, measure yourself against the commandments, take responsibility for your own life. Nonsense. You're a person, an individual—you spend your whole life working out your salvation, deciding what kind of person you want to be. The prophet has to be an apostle for thirty or forty years before he's prepared to be president of the Church. Just think about that. The Holy Ghost will help you, be a guide, of course, but you're responsible for your life, not the Holy Ghost, and don't you forget it, young man."

"Oh, I won't." And I wanted to say, "Just as long as it doesn't take all the fun out of life." But I didn't of course. Like Grandpa Hooper said, you have to go along if you want to get along, at least sometimes.

I knew what my funeral would be like. Probably last half an hour if I was lucky. Who would Frank and Lucille get to speak? Maybe they could con Tolson into reading a couple of sad, tragic poems, probably something from old Shakespeare, which would be about it. Or maybe Mrs. Clavir could talk about my potential as a pianist, if I'd only practiced about ten hours a day. I wasn't in the a cappella choir, but maybe they'd put together a quartet or maybe a duet.

"Great, just great."

• • •

I had to rest. I stuck the trenching tool in the side of the shaft and put my hands under my armpits and squeezed tight. I closed my eyes.

I knew that Mark and everybody would be charging up and down the halls at school yelling and talking, locker doors slamming shut, kids complaining about not having their homework done, pleading with their smart friends to let them copy theirs in class, and already talking about what was happening that weekend.

I wondered if Brooke had had her baby yet. It was going to be so prodigious to be an uncle, to see what my nephew looked like, maybe even like me just a little, or at least the Hooper side of the family, and hold him. I really wanted some kids of my own someday, but not too many, maybe two boys and a girl. I'd really start to study in college, get into medical or law school, or something, and two or three years after we were married, I'd come home from class one night because I'd been studying so hard. And my knock-out gorgeous wife who was a great cook would have my favorite supper ready, with flowers and lit candles on the table in our one-bedroom apartment, and she'd be all dressed up. And I'd kiss her and tell her how beautiful she looked. And after I sat down I'd ask her what was the big occasion.

And she'd smile and say, "Guess."

"Gee, honey, I don't know. Your Aunt Tilly died and left us a million bucks?"

"No, silly. She's not even sick. Guess again."

And I'd guess but not get it right, and she'd reach out and take my hand just like in the movies, and say, "You're going to be a father."

"A father? Are you sure? I can't believe it. How did that happen?"

Because I thought we were on the pill, but I wouldn't blame her or anything for maybe forgetting because she loved me so much. Or maybe it was an awesome spirit that was supposed to come to earth and we were supposed to provide it with a body, or this earthly tabernacle like Brother Glimmer said, so the pill didn't work. I'd tell her how wonderful that was and get up and hug her, like in the movies, and I'd ask her if it was going to be a boy or a girl.

"Silly, it's too early to tell."

But I'd know it would have to be a boy, and then she'd get bigger and bigger, which would be a little embarrassing, but all right because we were married. And I wouldn't let her lift anything heavy or do very much work because she was pregnant. And then one night about two in the morning, she'd say we had to go to the hospital. And the baby would be born with me right there in the delivery room, and I'd see it when it first came out and know it was my kid, and it would be a boy. We would already have picked a name, so we could call it by its name. And I'd have to phone Frank and Lucille, and Nate, Clay, and Brooke, and everybody, and say, "I'm a father." And everybody would say, "What? You are? Congratulations. That's wonderful. You'll make a great father." Except Lucille would say, "Well, welcome to the real world, Kyle. I've been looking forward to seeing you carry a diaper bag." And we'd have to bring it home and bring it up in righteousness, like you're supposed to I guess, but that would be okay. And I'd phone Mark and ask what was wrong with him because he'd have been married for two or three years too and going to school and his wife wasn't pregnant. But now maybe none of that would ever happen and I wouldn't ever be married or a father.

• • •

By noon I'd cut another two feet and had to cut my first footholds so I could reach the snow above my head. I cut both footholds on the same side and braced back against the shaft wall to dig. The stiff ski boots helped, but when I leaned against the snow the cold came through my parka, which was bad because it cooled my core temperature and could cause hypothermia. I cut off one side of the cardboard box and shoved it up under my parka. That helped.

"Maybe you are sort of smart, Hooper. Maybe."

I cut another hole higher up for the flashlight.

I had to keep talking to myself. It was so lonely in the half-darkness, like I lived in a world of shadows. I'd scraped the frost off the rearview mirror and looked at myself that morning. I was thinner, my eyes sinking back further into my head. At night in the darkness it was like I was the only person alive in the whole world. You had to be with other people every day to know you were alive.

Grandpa Hooper had told me a story once about six men trapped in a coal mine where he worked when he first got married. The rescue team figured out right where the men were, bored a hole down to them, and dropped a telephone so the team could talk to the trapped men and lower food and water. The miners talked to their families, friends, and the TV people. It would be so great if they located me with the aluminum poles and bored a hole and dropped a phone down so I could talk to people. Maybe they could drop down a camera so they could show pictures on TV of me digging myself out, my cave and everything. That would be pretty impressive, kind of heroic.

For lunch I fixed myself my last two tomato-lettuce-cheese-pickle sandwiches; I ate my last banana and drank a can of Pepsi. It was already the fourth day. They'd probably stopped searching. I really knew now that I'd have to dig myself out, unless I starved to death first, died of hypothermia, or the shaft caved in and I got smothered. My flashlight was getting dimmer too. I wished I could turn on the radio or had my iPod, but I didn't really want to listen to music. It would have been too strange down there. I wanted to hear voices.

Eating, I thought about Frank, who would have come home at least three days ago. He would have been in some big important late-night meeting in his hotel conference room or something in New York, and Nate would have called him.

"What? When did it happen? Kyle drove that Suburban up Silver Canyon? They're sure that's where he is? Yes, of course, of course. I'll be on the next plane. Let me talk to your mother."

"Frank, you're not home. Kyle's buried in an avalanche and you're not home. You weren't home when Trace died. Oh, Frank."

"I know, sweetheart. I'm sorry. I'm sorry. I'll be there as soon as I can."

And after he hung up Frank would turn to all the men sitting around the coffee table with all their important papers spread out and say, "My fifteen-year-old son Kyle was buried in an avalanche this morning driving up Silver Canyon to go skiing at a local ski resort. I have to leave as soon as I can get a plane. I'm sorry."

And all the high-powered New York business executives would be so helpful because they knew how important it was for Frank to get home, because they would think I was dead, and because he was such a nice guy. And he would tell them what a great kid I was and he couldn't believe I was dead, which I wasn't, of course.

After my Grandpa Hooper died, I missed Frank more when he went on his business trips. He was an easy guy to get along with. He didn't crack the whip like Lucille did. I just wanted to talk to Frank or maybe go skiing with him or something, and have him give me a hug sometimes like Grandpa Hooper used to. Maybe tell me what a great kid I was. Everybody said I was the only one of the four boys who looked like Frank, had his build, sandy hair, blue eyes, and big ears. Grandpa Hooper told me to try to get to know Frank. "He's okay. He's a good man. He'll figure out sooner or later that earning a million bucks isn't quite as important as he thinks it is. It takes us all a while to learn what's important in this life, and what isn't. Your grandma and I were struggling to make ends meet when he was a boy, so he didn't have much. Maybe that has something to do with his wanting to be rich. Of course, your mother likes to spend money, but then that's none of my business, I guess."

• • •

Later, working in the shaft, I still really thought an aluminum pole might break through into the shaft, and that I would have to drop the trenching tool and grab the pole fast before it got pulled back. It scared me to think I wouldn't be fast enough. But it still made me kind of smile when I thought what the ski-patrol guy would think when the pole suddenly got jerked out of his hands. He'd wet his pants or maybe faint, or start yelling, "He's here! Right here! He just jerked the pole out of my hand." And the guy next to him in the line would say, "You're nuts. That kid's been toast for four days." And the first guy would say, "No I'm not. Look. He's right under us." And he'd pull on the pole, and I'd pull back, and the other guy would start yelling that they'd found me, and all the lines would start yelling and come running over. It would be so worthy.

But then I knew they'd probably stopped searching for me anyway. Because what would be the point, except maybe to find my dead body, which made me sadder and even lonelier when I thought about it?

Seeing the mink was sort of encouraging. If he could stay alive under the avalanche, then maybe I could too. I hoped the mink would come back. I wished I had something to feed him. Mink liked fish and frogs.

I kept cutting the shaft, but my flashlight slowly went dim, and then went out, and I had to get a fresh set of batteries from the glove box. I only had one fresh set left, but I was still okay. Counting the cave, I'd cut fifteen feet. I should be out by Thursday anyway, even if the avalanche was thirty feet deep. It just couldn't be any deeper than that. I had the candle if I needed it.

But about two o'clock I hit a layer of long, broken-off spruce limbs that really slowed me down because they were four and five inches thick and I had to use the bow saw to cut them off on each side. My fingers were so numb I was afraid I might saw off two or three and not even know it until I saw the blood on the snow. But I'd already be dying by then, my blood all drained out. I almost said *damn* or *hell*, or something a lot worse like Grandpa said when he was really mad. But I didn't, because I'd promised God.

I started praying more, not out loud, just thinking the prayers and saying in the name of Jesus, amen. Because I knew that was important, but I wasn't sure exactly why. And I kept trying to figure out what faith was because you had to have faith or nothing worked. And I decided it was believing you could do something and doing it, even though you didn't really know you could. Or you didn't know something was true, but you just believed it and you lived that way. So faith gave you more possibilities than always having to know because there were just a lot of things you couldn't know.

I wanted to ask Lucille about it. She was always talking about faith and how you had to have faith, faith in everything, yourself, other people, the government, the mechanic who fixed your car, faith in yourself even. But mostly you had faith in God and in the Church. Because you couldn't always know things; you just had to have faith, believe, or you wouldn't ever do anything, wouldn't act. She was always telling me that I tried her faith, which I guess I did, sort of maybe. In our family prayers she'd pray for me sometimes; of course, she prayed for everybody, the whole world, Mark, even Trace after he died that he'd be okay and know how much we loved him. But mostly she prayed for me, asking the Lord to guide and direct me, and for the Holy Ghost to protect me and help me to have at least a little sense and to keep the commandments.

I'd open my eyes to look at her, and she'd look so serious, her eyes shut tight, her knees on the floor, leaning forward on her chair, her head bowed. It was kind of embarrassing being prayed for when Mark was there kneeling around the table with us sometimes. But he didn't seem to mind that she prayed for him too. She didn't pray that he'd join the Church of course, because she couldn't be that obvious, but that he'd just be blessed in general. She even prayed that Mark and I would finish our Eagles, because Mark was a Second Class too. We went on all the camping trips, but getting all the badges was boring after we turned fourteen.

And Lucille was always after me to get my patriarchal blessing too.

"If anybody needs one you do. A blessing is a great help. It gives your whole life direction. Your brothers and your sister all have their blessings. It's a wonderful thing to know what the Lord wants you to do. The patriarch places his hands on your head and speaks the mind of the Lord for you because he's inspired. It's a sacred experience."

Yeah, sure. I had about all the direction I could deal with. I'd read Trace's blessing. You had to do all these things, keep all the commandments, go on a mission and preach the gospel to the whole world, get married in the temple, raise a righteous posterity, sit in the councils of the Church, whatever that was supposed to mean. And then you got all these blessings, and went to the celestial kingdom and finally became a god. I just wanted to put it off for a while, not have to think about all those things and tie myself down while I was still young and could still enjoy myself a little, at least. Brother Glimmer told us in seminary that during pioneer days they'd announce mission calls during general conference in the Salt Lake tabernacle. You'd be sitting there with your wife and eight kids and you'd hear your name called to serve in China for about five years, and your wife would about faint because how was she going to feed all those kids while you were gone preaching the gospel? Really radical.

And I wanted to ask Lucille, "What about Trace? He died. What about all the great things he was supposed to do?" But I already knew the answer to that one because of this lesson old Brother Glimmer had hit us with in seminary. If you died young and righteous, you did all of these things in the next life, like getting married and having kids and everything. Dying wasn't really that bad. So I didn't ask Lucille. I didn't want to have to listen to her explain all about eternity and all the blessings the righteous got, and all that stuff again.

• • •

Despite the cardboard inside my parka, the cold still crept into my body from leaning back against the side of the shaft. I was so cold, tired, and hungry when I quit that night that I could hardly climb down out of the shaft. I decided to eat more. I needed the energy to keep working hard and punch the shaft through. I knew that if I didn't do that by tomorrow, or Thursday at the latest, I wouldn't need the food.

I opened the big can of pork and beans with the Scout knife and ate half of them. I drank two cans of pop. Between bites I sipped the little bit of pickle juice left in the bottle. It wasn't very nutritious, but it helped get the beans down. It was the first time I'd felt full in quite a while. I just had to be out by Thursday.

I'd dreamed about Mark the night before. We'd been on

a date with these terrific girls, and I was flying a plane, not driving a car, and we crashed in the snow-covered mountains, but we weren't killed, just sat there in the plane freezing and wondering what to do. Grandpa Hooper had told me a story once about a soccer team whose plane crashed in the Peruvian Alps, and after about a week the starving survivors voted to eat their dead friends. One of the soccer players was a medical student or something, and he cut them up in thin slices, so they wouldn't be too hard to eat, which would be pretty ultimate. I pictured my friends in my mind. I knew if I was in a plane crash I couldn't eat any of them, no matter how hungry I was, especially if they were girls. I knew that Mark wouldn't either, if he was with me. He just wasn't that kind of kid. In history we studied about the Donner Party that got caught in the Sierra Nevada Mountains with their covered wagons all winter and became cannibals. But when they cut up the people who died, they wrote the person's name on the package so you wouldn't be eating a family member and not know it.

When we got out of class, Mark said, "That'd be so gross."

"But still kind of considerate when you think about it, under the circumstances."

"Oh, sure. You have my Aunt Tilly for supper, and I'll have your Aunt Penny. We can compare recipes. Hooper, sometimes you're so dense."

Mark had started coming to sacrament meeting with us. He even wore his suit with a white shirt and a tie, which was a bad sign. Every Sunday Bishop Goodmer always shook Mark's hand, put his other hand on his shoulder, called him Brother Mark, which was another bad sign. Next he'd have old Mark in his office for one of those little chats of his. Warning Mark about what he was getting into didn't help. Mark said he'd asked his mom to come with him to church, but she said after working six days a week, sometimes seven, she needed a little time off. But she wanted him to keep going. One night Mark's mom phoned Lucille to thank her for feeding Mark supper so often and letting him study at our house at night. I was sitting at the kitchen table eating a piece of pie with vanilla ice cream.

"Mark's a wonderful friend for Kyle. We're pleased to have him in our home. He's no trouble at all." Afterward Lucille told me that Mark's mom appreciated our taking Mark to church because that was something he needed since his dad died.

"Oh, sure, Mom."

"What do you mean by that, young man."

"Oh, nothing."

• • •

After I ate half the can of pork and beans, I climbed out of the Suburban and put three beans on a log above Crystal Creek for the mink. I didn't know if mink liked beans, but I wanted to feed him something. He might be hungry. Maybe fish and frogs were hard to catch in the winter.

Standing at the Suburban door, I turned and spit just to see if it would crackle and freeze in the air like with the miner in Alaska, but it didn't. I decided it had to be at least seventy-five degrees below zero for that to happen. It wasn't that cold, at least not yet.

Later, wrapped in the quilt, I began to shiver again. But I could stop if I tried real hard, tightened my whole body and clenched my teeth to keep them from chattering, trying to sleep. The paramedics said uncontrolled shivering was an early sign of hypothermia. Even under the quilt and held under my arms, my hands were still stiff and cold. My gloves were getting worn, my shriveled fingers and toes turning white. I had to keep taking off my boots and rubbing my feet so they wouldn't stay numb. I was glad my parka and gloves were Gore-Tex. If I got wet I'd catch pneumonia or something worse, like the hypothermia taking over really fast. The air force colonel Grandpa Hooper had told me about who lived in the bamboo cage in Vietnam had gotten dysentery, boils, malaria, and other diseases, and lost ninety pounds because they didn't give him enough to eat, but he never gave up.

"I want to run. I want to just run and run, and never stop, just run."

I didn't mean to say that; it just came out. I ran cross-country on the track team. Running was so great, in just my running shorts, no shirt, nothing else except track shoes, not even socks, my whole body loose, feeling the air touch me. My legs, arms, feet, shoulders, even my head, moving perfectly, feeling the heat, breathing, my body oiled. My stride so smooth, perfect, loose, not watching the runners ahead of me, just running myself, my blood warm, giving it everything I had at the kick. Just me, more aware of my whole body than I'd ever been before in my whole life, even my long heavy hair, so prodigious.

Lucille came to all my meets, brought all the family she could drag along. I never won, but I'd hear her yelling and Nate, Clay, Brooke, Jed, and Frank too. And afterward she'd hug me, even though I was all sweaty, and then stand back and say, "You're beautiful. Isn't he beautiful?" And I was. At least that's the way I felt.

We'd all gone to Trace's tennis games. Trace was Mr. Perfection, won nearly every game he ever played. We'd all be yelling, and I'd look up, and Lucille's eyes were full of tears she was so happy, which was okay. It didn't bother me too much. Trace *was* great, all dressed in white like he was going to be baptized right after the game, at least a dozen terrific girls sitting together at every match, cheering every time he made one of those great overhand shots of his, the other guy not coming within a mile. Trace already had three universities interested in him, including Stanford, before he got so sick.

Of course Lucille was always on my case about the Word of Wisdom and not polluting the body with drugs, alcoholic beverages, cigarettes, tea, or coffee, although like I said she wasn't a fanatic on Coke and other caffeine-laden beverages, so she didn't take that small joy out of my life.

"Your body is the temple of your spirit, young man. The Word of Wisdom is the Lord's law of health. I hope you understand that. The Lord promises treasures of knowledge to those who obey."

Except I found that didn't work on math, physics, and chemistry exams, because I'd tried that a couple of times when I didn't study, really had faith but still got C's both times and not my usual B- or a B, if I was lucky. I guessed I didn't have enough faith. I wanted to ask Lucille how that all worked, but decided I probably shouldn't, under the circumstances.

And when Lucille would ask me if I understood the blessings that came with obeying the Word of Wisdom, I'd say, "Sure, Mom, I know all about it."

"Well, just be sure you do."

Lucille gave her family home evening lesson on the Word of Wisdom annually of course. And she gave a presentation to the Relief Society, which Bishop Goodmer saw, and was so impressed with. And he told the other two bishops of the wards meeting in our chapel, and they asked Lucille to put together a presentation for all three wards on that particular subject because the sex education thing had been so successful. And of course old President Smyles picked up on it, so she had to do it in the other chapels, with a bishop leading the discussion, like before. And I had to go along to help with all the technical stuff so it would all get pounded into my head again and I'd become reasonable. Reasonable? What mother would make her son do something so lugubrious? But Mark came to help me, which I appreciated. Of course he thought the presentation was very interesting.

"Oh, sure, just delightful."

"You're lucky," he said afterward, sitting there eating a big ice cream sundae with topping, whipped cream, and nuts, which after the meetings the stake presidency and the three bishoprics in white aprons always served just to calm the kids' nerves. "Think of all those kids at school who drink, smoke pot, and shoot up."

"You and Lucille."

Mark was very concerned about staying in shape. He was the best hundred-yard man at Jefferson High. Of course, I ran cross-country, and the best cross-country man in the state was on our team, a senior named Chris Swifter. So much better than me it was pathetic. But his folks bought him a motorcycle, and he quit, said he didn't need to run anymore. His folks didn't want him to have a bike, but they said if he earned half the money, they'd pay the rest. They didn't think he'd do it, but he did. His dad was a surgeon at Silver City Hospital, and every time a motorcycle accident victim was brought into the emergency room, his dad phoned Chris to come and see the guy. It was part of the deal, because his mom and dad thought that seeing all these mangled bodies, the guys screaming if they were still conscious, would scare Chris and he wouldn't want a bike. Because he was a doctor, his dad could take him right in where they were working on the biker. Before he quit the track team, Chris told us all about it.

"You should see some of those guys, hear them screaming, really gross. They got broken bones, sometimes the bones sticking out. Big cuts, with blood all over. Big burns everywhere from rolling half a mile down the freeway, half their clothes ripped off, even their T-shirts and shorts sometimes. If the biker was out of surgery when I got there, my dad took me up to his hospital room. The guy would be all bandaged like a mummy. He'd maybe have arms and legs in splints and raised up with pulleys. All you could see through the bandages was his mouth and eyes, maybe his nose. They can't get up to go to the bathroom or anything."

But Chris still bought his bike. Seeing all the mangled victims didn't bother him. And then three months later he'd sold it and was back on the track team. We were coming back from a practice run and just coming into the gym when Todd Dimmer asked Chris why. Chris stopped and turned. We all stopped because we all wondered about that.

"Well, because biking wasn't as much fun as I thought it would be. I'd rather run cross-country. Biking's okay, but it's like you're part of a machine, not yourself, like you're made of metal too. Running's more personal, not noisy. Clean. You feel who you are more. You're not so blown away. You don't get hurt either." Chris paused, looking down at us. He was the tallest kid on the team. "Last week my dad told me some kid over at Mountain High School crashed into a truck on his bike going eighty, got all smashed up, and they had to cut off both his feet just above the ankles."

"Gee, Chris, that's too bad," Glen Meekly said. "Is he going to be okay?"

"Okay? Sure. He's going to be just great, Meekly. Not a thing to worry about. Take his girl to the school dance next week. Meekly, you're an idiot. You'll always be an idiot."

"Gee, Chris, Meekly was just asking."

"You're an idiot too, Limply. You're both idiots. You're all idiots."

We didn't stay in the showers that day, didn't horse around, have wet towel fights or anything. Head bent under the hot water hitting you, soap suds running down your body, down your legs, down between your toes. You didn't want to think about what it would be like if your feet were cut off too. You got out, dried off, dressed, and went home, not even talking, walking down the hall wiggling your toes in your shoes just to be sure they were there.

• • •

I clamped my jaws against the shivering. I felt like I'd lived down here in the cold and darkness for years. Being cramped and bent over made me feel like a mole, only worse. I worried about another avalanche hitting the basin, but I still believed God wouldn't do that to me, because I was trying to have all this faith.

I knew that all I had to do was turn on the engine and get the heater going to get warm, melt the thick frost. It was a great heater. But I knew if I did this just for five minutes, I'd probably doze off and die of carbon-monoxide poisoning. But I had to get warm somehow. I wasn't going to make it if I didn't. I was going to get hypothermia; my fingers and toes would turn black with frostbite. I wouldn't be able to dig anymore, and I'd just slowly freeze.

"If only I had Grandpa's hose, I could dig a tunnel to the back of the Suburban, attach it to the exhaust pipe, and run it down into Crystal Creek. Then I could run the engine and get warm. If I had the hose I know I could do it. Damn. Oh, I'm sorry. I won't swear anymore, ever, like I promised."

I knew I had the roll of heavy aluminum foil, but that wouldn't be strong enough to make a hose. I could seal it with duct tape, but it would still collapse, and tape wouldn't stick anyway because of the cold. I kept thinking about my resources. I needed Grandpa Hooper; he could always figure how to make something work. I had most of the cardboard box left, an empty plastic milk jug, the empty pop cans, the bean can after I ate the rest of the beans, duct tape, a roll of wire, and whatever fabric or metal I could strip from the inside of the Suburban, and the foil. But I knew that wasn't enough.

Falling asleep, I thought about bears hibernating in caves all winter. I knew their breathing slowed down and they lived on their body fat. Too bad I couldn't do that because then I'd just have to wait for the spring thaw.

Fifth Day, Wednesday

I ate the last of the pork and beans for breakfast and drank a Coke. I needed carbohydrates to keep up my body heat. We'd studied all about them in my health class. I didn't remember if beans had carbohydrates. I knew I should have saved some of the beans for later, but I was too hungry. I had to have food, or I was going to get so weak I couldn't dig. I'd just curl tight into myself, shrivel up, my bones pushing my skin tight. All I had left was pop and some mayonnaise and catsup.

I looked at the Coke can in my hand. Grandpa Hooper had soldered Coke cans together to build a lawn chair. It was kind of a joke, but you could sit in it. He called it his Coke chair.

I tipped the can to look at the two ends. If I had a soldering iron, solder, and a power supply, I could cut out the ends with the Scout-knife can opener, solder the cans together, and make a hose for the exhaust. But even if I could duct-tape the cans together, I'd need about a hundred cans to make a hose long enough. I had eighteen, and if the avalanche had punched a hole in the muffler or broken the exhaust pipe, it wouldn't help anyway. I'd still be toast.

Grandpa Hooper was great to teach me how to build things, always telling me stories about his life, but he never told me any stories about battles and men getting wounded and killed in Korea, what it was like hollering "Medic! Medic!" while trying to stop a soldier from bleeding to death with his arm shot off or blinded in both eyes and screaming, "I can't see, I can't see!" Or maybe wounded in the chest, blood coming out of his nose, and the soldier dying so he just looks up at you like in the war flicks. And he tells you to write to his mom, and then his head turns, so you know he's dead. But his eyes don't close, so you have to close them with your fingers, and then you stick his rifle in the ground with the bayonet and hang his helmet on it so the stretcher bearers don't miss him. So horrendous.

"I've seen too much of war, son, too much blood and dying. Best forget it, I guess. Your grandmother was always trying to get me to go to church again, but maybe I saw too much, and I'm not proud of some of the things I did. But I want you to go to church. A boy needs to believe in God; that's important. You keep your nose clean. Do what the Church says. Those commandments are there for a purpose. You go on a mission too, like your dad and your brothers. I didn't go, but you go." And then Grandpa turned and looked up at the sky and the mountains, and was quiet for a few minutes. "A lot of good men lost their lives over there in Korea. Seen men break down and cry when their buddies got killed. Saw a lot of heroes too, and they never got any medals. Ran into a few bastards, but then you expect that in the army."

Grandpa Hooper's favorite swear word was in the dictionary and meant illegitimate, so it wasn't really swearing, and he used it only when he got really riled up about somebody. He had all kinds of interesting adjectives he attached to that particular word, like "sorry-assed," kind of his favorite, and "dumb," "stupid," "hopeless," "ignorant," "miserable," just plain "sorry," and "eighteen-carat."

After English class one day when we'd been talking about adjectives, which were helping words, I told Mark that when Tolson was asking for good examples, I was going to tell her some of Grandpa Hooper's helping words when he swore, but just when I was going to raise my hand the bell rang.

"Oh, sure, Hooper, why not? Tolson would really have appreciated your contribution."

"But they're great examples."

"Give me a break. You'd have been down in Jagger's office in thirty seconds flat."

"But Tolson might have liked some examples from real life. All the examples the kids gave were pretty lame."

"About as lame as you are, Hooper."

"Ah, I don't know."

"Well, I do."

"It's not exactly nefarious."

"There you go again. *Nefarious*? What's that supposed to mean?"

"It's a good word. It means bad."

"Bad? Why don't you just say bad then?"

"Nefarious sounds better?"

Mark just shook his head. "Sounds better."

I liked to repeat interesting words to myself, over and over again, just to hear their sounds, words like "sextuplicate," which isn't even about sex, but is kind of musical.

I liked Grandpa Hooper's favorite swear word, the sound of it, with the right adjective attached. I thought about using it around Lucille sometime just to get a rise out of her, but I knew she'd probably kill me. I didn't want to push her too far. You had to know just which buttons to press and when. But if I did happen to slip, I could always say it was in the dictionary, so it must be an okay word. I'd even go get the dictionary and show her that it meant the same as illegitimate. But I knew how far I'd get with that one.

• • •

Sitting there in the cab wrapped in my quilt, I said, "Think, Kyle, think." Grandpa Hooper always said to think when you

were in a tough spot, Lucille too, even when you weren't. What
else did I have to make an exhaust hose? I knew I had to be
able to extend the cans somehow. I'd have to take my chances
on the muffler and exhaust pipe not being broken. I had to
get warm or I wasn't going to make it. Turning I saw the roll
of heavy aluminum foil in the box. I could join the cans with
sections of rolled foil to make a tube so that each can gave me
about a foot of hose. But if I joined the foil to the cans with
duct tape, how was I going to make it stick? I thought about
that and decided I could heat it with the candle to make it stick.
It might work. I knew I had to try it.

"Thanks, Grandpa." I said that out loud, but I knew I was
figuring things out myself too, because you had to do that. I
knew the Holy Ghost must be helping me too because he was
supposed to inspire you and everything.

I'd have to dig a tunnel to the back of the Suburban, which
would take at least a day. But I had to do it. I'd thought about
turning on the engine to see if the pipe or muffler was broken.
But I wouldn't know if the exhaust was coming from a break
or just out the end of the pipe.

I had to get warm. I had to recharge the battery too. If
it went dead, I'd just have the flashlight and the candle. If I
could run the engine and keep the Suburban battery charged,
I'd be able to turn on the inside and dash lights more, run the
heater and get warm, and listen to the radio too. It would be so
great to hear voices and know other people were alive and not
just me. I'd use a lot of my flashlight battery time digging the
tunnel, but I didn't have a choice.

I spent the morning cutting the tunnel. It was easier than
working in the shaft; I didn't run into any spruce limbs or
rocks. I kept worrying about Lucille. I'd been in the avalanche
five days. She'd have to know I was dead, but she wouldn't
want to. I didn't want her to worry about me like she did about
Trace, walking around the house whispering, "No, no, no. Oh,

please, Lord, not Trace, not Trace. He's such a wonderful boy. He wants to go on a mission. He's been studying Chinese in high school for three years. He's so talented. Please, Lord."

It was like she was pleading, asking the Lord in our family prayers to spare Trace, but still she had faith, even after Trace died she still went to church, bore her testimony, talked about the Lord in his wisdom and all that stuff, which I guessed was what faith was. What would she pray about me when she first heard I was buried? Probably, "Kyle has a lot to learn, Lord; he isn't ready like his brother Trace. I need him here. He's so young. He needs to go on his mission." Or something like that, like I was just a kid. She always said she had to finish raising me, which she did, sort of anyway, I guess, except it was kind of embarrassing because I was almost sixteen and should have been raised by then, I thought.

You could send in your missionary papers three months before you turned eighteen, so I could get my call even before I graduated from Jefferson High. I'd be ordained an elder, and the girls probably wouldn't even date me, would start calling me elder, even the nonmember girls because they'd know. No girl would let me kiss her because she'd probably think it would weaken my testimony, and it would be on a long list of things I couldn't do anyway, including even holding hands. All the called missionaries would probably even have to start wearing a white shirt and tie to school, a dark suit and black shoes too probably, so we'd look like morticians, and all the other kids would know, and we'd have to be all righteous and pious. We'd have to go to the temple to take out our endowments, which meant you learned all about the creation and made all these promises about living a righteous life forever, and start wearing temple garments. And wouldn't that be sweet in the locker room, but at least they looked like shorts and a T-shirt, and the nonmember guys would be all respectful because you explained they were sacred. But the guys would want to know all about the temple, which would be a teaching opportunity, as Lucille calls it. All really radical stuff.

• • •

When I reached the back of the Suburban, I turned off the flashlight because I had the back-up lights. I cleared the exhaust pipe and then turned on the engine to see if the exhaust would come out, or if the pipe or muffler was broken. It did. So copacetic. "Thank you, God. I really mean it. Thank you." I made my cave longer so I'd have a place to run my hose down to Crystal Creek. I cut a six-inch-deep ditch for the hose.

I was really beat after I got the cave dug out. I knew I was getting weaker because I didn't have enough to eat. I'd seen a documentary about an injured mountain climber whose rope broke and he fell over a ledge. The two guys climbing with him couldn't find him because of a snow storm, and they thought he was dead anyway, but he'd dug a snow cave so he didn't freeze. He still had his pack. Because he had a broken leg, he couldn't get into his sleeping bag, so he covered himself with it and his tent and slept on his pad. The next morning he wrapped the pad around his broken leg for a splint and tied it. He cut up the floor of his tent to make a pad for his good knee and started crawling down the trail his buddies had left after the snow storm quit, dragging his broken leg. All he had left to eat was one chocolate bar. He ate snow for water. He cried a lot and wet himself, was in awesome pain, but he kept going. So worthy. His biggest fear was dying alone. Having somebody with him when he died made his dying important or something. He didn't have a phone, so he couldn't call his girlfriend or mother or somebody and say he was dying and they'd say how sorry they were and ask what happened.

"Well, at least I don't have a broken leg, at least not yet."

I cut the ends out of the pop cans with the Scout knife. I'd poured the full cans into the milk bottle so I'd still have that to drink. I had to take my gloves off to work. I lit the candle to warm my fingers. I was careful not to bend the cans. I decided to make two foil tubes for strength, one to fit inside the other. I couldn't seal them with the duct tape, even when I heated it with the candle, so I crimped the ends. I had to keep thinking.

Knowing I might die anyway didn't scare me so much, like it did before. Sleeping in the same room with Trace, talking to him, watching him be so sick, getting weaker and weaker all the time, and then dying helped because if it was something he could do, I could too, maybe. Dying was just something that happened to you, wasn't it, or something you just did, everybody did? What was there to be scared of? Trace was sad he had to die, but he didn't complain or get mad at God. Trace had faith.

Lucille talked to him about what it would be like in heaven; Grandma and Grandpa Hooper would be there, all the other relatives who'd perished, going back hundreds of years, and his high school friends who'd died, and God and Jesus. And Trace would be all healed, have his perfect body in heaven, and we'd all be there someday, be a family, and he could get married, have kids, and nobody would ever have to die again or be sick, forever. Sitting on the edge of his bed, Lucille held his hands, reaching up to smooth back his hair, kissing him.

Trace cried at night sometimes, quiet tears shiny on his face in the moonlight from the window, like he was just crying for himself because he was so sad about having to die, not because he was scared or mad.

"It's so beautiful outside, Kyle. Really beautiful." Trace said that one night when I was already in bed. The lights off, he often sat at the window in his wheelchair looking out, the backyard, trees, and other houses moonlit. "It's like I've never really seen things before, Kyle. I guess you don't, do you, until you're really sick and not going to get better? You just want

to go on seeing and feeling and not have to stop. You have to
pray a lot."

Lying in bed seeing Trace sitting there silhouetted against
the window, I didn't know what to say. I wanted to be all
commodious, but I didn't know how. If I froze to death, starved
to death, or died of hypothermia, I believed that Trace and
Grandpa and Grandma would be waiting for me somewhere,
maybe on another planet. I really believed that; they just had
to be. But I wasn't giving up; I couldn't. I wanted to be alive;
I knew what that was like. I couldn't really imagine myself
dead, although I knew you had to die sometime, of course, but
only when you were really old. And I didn't want to make my
family all sad.

• • •

I had to keep warming my fingers over the candle, but be
careful not to burn them and not know it. I put a scratch in
the dashboard for every day, but I didn't worry about what
day it was; it didn't matter. I just had to keep working. I kept
thinking about Lucille. Sleep wasn't important.

I used the duct tape as a pad around the foil at each end of
the can and then tightened it down with a loop of wire. I had
to be careful not to bend the can. The tape did stick a little,
which helped seal the connection. I started laying my hose
down toward the creek. I knew I wouldn't be able to build the
whole hose and then pull it down to the creek without breaking
it. I knew I was thinking ahead, sort of. Building the cabin,
if I wired a switch or light wrong, stripped the threads on a
piece of plastic pipe, broke a piece of expensive tile, or did
something else stupid, and got mad, Grandpa Hooper said,
"Back off a minute, Kyle. Think about what you're doing. The
only way to learn is to keep trying."

Cutting the shiny foil, seeing my hands, I felt how dirty

I was. I didn't like to be dirty. The snow was full of dirt. A long, hot shower would be so great. Lucille was always telling me not to empty both tanks, not take every drop of hot water in the house. I ran my tongue across my teeth. I needed to brush my teeth. Girls told me I had a nice smile. Girls I knew from school waved when I was out running, getting in shape for cross-country. Just in shorts, no shirt, my whole body felt loose, whole, no parts missing, gleaming with sweat. I always waved back to girls, slowed down, ran in place, so I could talk to them. I knew the girls liked to be close to me, the beads of sweat running down over my muscles, my lungs taking deep, long breaths, sort of panting, feeling so basic. Sometimes a girl reached up to touch my arm or my chest with her cool fingers or maybe her whole hand. And I'd reach out with just one finger and touch her on the nose. They like to be touched on the nose. Or I'd kiss the tip of my index finger and put it on her lips, because Lucille said there was plenty of time for kissing when I got back from my mission, but she couldn't complain about that because it wasn't really kissing, just touching, sort of.

"Nice," the girl would say, or something like that, or maybe, "You're sweet, do you know that?" And I'd say, "Yes." And she'd smile and maybe wink, her perfume smelling like she was a big flower or something, maybe a whole bouquet, her lips and eyes shining, a real lovely. And I'd smile. But that wouldn't happen if you played football because all those other guys would be around too, and you'd be out on the field, dressed in a uniform, pads three inches thick, and girls wouldn't be allowed on the field anyway, of course. So you couldn't be alone and just stop and run in place and talk and be close enough so she could touch your gleaming body, which she couldn't do anyway because of all that football armor.

I needed to have a really sweet car, not just my Suburban, so girls would want me to drive them home from school, maybe a luxurious convertible with the top down, and I'd have four or five girls in the car and take them all home one at a time. Before Mark got his license, he and I used to ride our bikes to the Silver City car dealerships to look at all the new models and pick up brochures and talk about the car we were both going to buy someday when we were rich, which was a red Jaguar XK convertible. We'd sometimes sit in a display car, hold onto the steering wheel, breathe in that new-car smell, the best smell in the world, till some smart-assed salesman would come up and say, "You planning to buy it, kid? Get lost." And I wished Frank were a multimillionaire, and I'd tell him I wanted this red Jag convertible and he'd say, "Sure, son, why not, you're a great kid, you got to enjoy life while you're young." And he'd make me out a personal check for maybe sixty thousand right there. And when the salesman asked his dumb-assed question, if I was buying, I'd say, "Sure," whip out my wallet and hand him the check just to see the look on his face when he read my dad's signature and started calling me sir.

• • •

Fumbling, my fingers so cold I could hardly make them work, even when I warmed them over the candle, I attached the last can to the aluminum tube and wired it to the exhaust pipe. I covered the ditch with spruce branches to protect my hose and then covered that with snow, packing it down just a little. Completely beat, really wasted, I blew out the candle, which was down to about four inches now, and crawled back up the tunnel.

Sitting behind the steering wheel, the ceiling light on, I closed my eyes tight. "Oh, God, please let it work. Please, please. In the name of Jesus, amen." I'd never prayed like that before, except maybe when I prayed that Trace wouldn't die, really prayed, like I was really talking to somebody.

I pulled off my worn gloves. I knew I had to have faith.

"I have faith. I have faith. I have to have faith." I turned the key. The engine caught. I listened. The engine ran smoothly. I waited. It kept running. I took my thumb and finger away from the key.

"Thank you."

I kept smelling for exhaust fumes, but my nose was so cold it was hard to smell. If the Suburban filled with carbon monoxide, I'd turn off the engine, and just take it from there. But as cold, hungry, and weak as I was, I knew I couldn't last very long.

I waited to turn on the heater. No point in having cold air blowing on me. I waited. I knew I was getting better at figuring out things, the Holy Ghost helping me of course, and all the things Grandpa Hooper and Lucille taught me of course, but mainly it was just me. I kept smelling for exhaust fumes. None. Lucille would be impressed. She was always saying I couldn't wait five minutes for anything.

I reached up and turned on the heater. I felt the warm air. I held my hands down by the heater. The air got warmer. I turned the heater on full blast. My hands hurt, but the heat felt so wonderful. I'd never felt anything so wonderful in my whole life, so inestimable, so worthy. I closed my eyes to feel it better, just feel the warmth creeping into my burning hands. I rubbed my nose on the sleeve of my parka, shook my head, squeezed my eyes tight against the tears. My hands stung, but I didn't pull them away.

"Thank you, God. Thank you, thank you, thank you. And thanks, Grandpa Hooper, too."

The heat felt so good, but being warm made me feel dirty because I could feel my skin and smell my dirty clothes. The frozen snow was full of dirt. I'd never been so dirty in my whole life. I didn't ever like to feel dirty. A hot shower was so great, feeling the hot water coming down over the top of my head, shampooing my hair, rinsing it, soaping up, watching the soap washing down off my chest, stomach, and legs, so I was standing there shiny clean, face raised into the hot water till I had to turn it off. I'd reach for a fresh towel, smelling how clean it was, and I'd shave even though I didn't really have to, and put on my special aftershave. I'd put on clean shorts and a T-shirt and comb my clean hair, and put on a clean shirt, jeans, and socks, everything clean. Girls like you to look fresh and clean, like you did it all for them, just standing there shining. So great to feel clean, so inestimable.

"I've got to get out of here. I just got to."

If I died I'd miss my junior and senior years of high school. That made me sad. It was going to be so great to be a senior finally, go to all the parties, dances, and games, and not take any hard classes, except maybe English, which I liked sort of, so I'd have lots of time to enjoy myself. Of course, I'd have to get past Lucille on that one. She was always checking what classes I took and my grades. I could just hear her after looking at my senior schedule.

"Well, Kyle, this is a heavy load for a senior—film history, yearbook, lifetime sports, coed basketball/volleyball. You do have English Literature. That's a step in the right direction. What about advanced classes in chemistry, physics, math, and perhaps even biology. You did manage to get B's in the sophomore and junior classes. Don't you think you should improve your skills? You might even get into State."

"Come on, Mom, I've filled all my graduation requirements. I've worked hard. I just want to relax and enjoy life a little."

"I know, Kyle, I know how hard you've worked. But perhaps now you should concentrate on some really tough classes your senior year, maybe an AP class or two. You've got the brains. We know that. It's just a matter of using them. Mark earns almost straight A's in hard classes. Why don't you follow his example?"

"Oh, sure. All I need is another example."

And then I knew she'd make me revise my whole schedule, except for English. I liked English. In Tolson's class we'd been reading *The Scarlet Letter* about old Hester Prynne, who had to wear a big red A for adultery because she'd been sleeping with the Puritan pastor and got pregnant, but I figured it should have been an F for fornication. Because she wasn't married, was she, so it couldn't be adultery, could it, which got me thinking. I was going to mention this fact in class, but decided maybe Tolson wouldn't want to have this big discussion on the difference between fornication and adultery.

After class I told Mark we ought to go talk to old Principal Jagger and suggest that he set up a special student committee to make letters for kids to wear, except not the letter A, because kids couldn't do that.

"What are you talking about this time, Hooper? Sometimes you don't make very much sense. In fact, most of the time?"

"Well, they'd have letters like J for junkie, STD for sexually transmitted diseases like syphilis, gonorrhea, AIDS, and all that stuff, JO for juvenile offender, C for cheater, DUI for driving under the influence, S for shoplifter, GMGP for got my girlfriend pregnant, H for harlot, and W for whoremonger—nailing those guys would really cheer up old Lucille. Kids will have to pick up their letters in the morning and wear them all day."

"You're crazy, Hooper. No kid's going to tell what they did. Harlot? What's that supposed to mean? Harlot? Where did you find that word, in some old dictionary?"

"It's a good word. People used to use it all the time, especially in the Bible."

"I'll bet."

"Kids wouldn't have to tell the letters they were supposed to wear. Jagger would have a certified list in his office. Doctors, the county health office, and the juvenile court could submit names, even parents if they wanted to, and kids who knew what was going on and wanted to help their friends stop. Kids would have to come to the office every morning and pick up their letter to pin on. It would really make school more interesting to see what letters different kids were wearing. And it would help cut down on all that bad stuff because kids wouldn't want to wear a letter so that everybody would know. It would be very educational."

"Yeah, and you could wear N for nut."

"Come on, it would work. Mark, you just don't have any imagination."

"Well, tomorrow in English bring up your brilliant idea. Tolson will probably send you to counseling, if the class, including the girls, doesn't toss you out the window first so you can suffer a tragic death."

"Well, at least you have to admit it's an original idea."

"No, I don't."

"Grandpa Hooper told me that when his older brother was wounded in Germany during World War II and was in the hospital in England, they had a special ward for soldiers who were being treated for STD, only they called it venereal disease. All the soldiers had to wear red robes with VD in foot-high letters painted on the back in white. So Hester Prynne wasn't the only one to have to do something like that."

"Hooper, you're not just nuts, you're crazy."

"It would make school so interesting. You could look around and see who was wearing what new letter every morning."

"Oh, sure. You could keep a check-off list."

After Grandpa told me the army story, I thought about what it would be like to walk around the hospital wearing one of those red robes with everybody seeing you. Grandpa said that was where whoring got you and that some of those soldiers had wives and children back in the States, which was hard to believe. And if a soldier had VD it went on his army records, so that wherever he went in the army the officers knew. I knew *whore* was a word, but I'd never heard *whoring* before. I figured it was a gerund because of the *ing* ending; I knew it wasn't a participle because it didn't have a *to* in front of it like *to whore*. Whoring was kind of musical; somebody should put it in a song or something.

But I didn't say anything about G for gay. I called a kid at school a faggot once, which was a slight error on my part. Lucille came down on me like a ton of bricks.

"Faggot? What's that supposed to mean?"

"I don't know. Gay I guess. It's the word kids use."

"Is this boy a human being? I mean does he walk and talk, laugh, cry maybe sometimes, eat lunch in the cafeteria?"

"Sure. I guess."

"You guess. Well, for your information, Kyle, being homosexual, or gay if you prefer, isn't a crime. Some males choose to be gay. Others are born gay; that's their sexual orientation. Many would prefer not to be gay, but there isn't a lot they can do about it. It's a biological characteristic. Being gay in the Church is extremely difficult, if not impossible, because everything is about family, in this life and the next. And some chaste youth who think they might be gay, but don't want to be, become elders and go on missions and believe if they dedicate themselves to the Lord they won't be gay anymore when they come home. But that doesn't work. At one time some bishops used to advise gay returned missionaries to marry because that would cure them, as if being gay were a disease. But that didn't work either, of course, and bishops stopped doing that, thank heaven. How many broken marriages, broken hearts, and tragedy did that cause? So you need to think about that, young man. Gays can have a temple recommend as long as they're chaste, just like heterosexuals, and be active in the Church, and go to BYU, if they want to. And don't let me hear you use that word again, or *homo* or *queer*, or you and I are going to have some very lengthy discussions, which I don't think will be particularly pleasant."

"Okay, okay, Mom. I understand."

"I certainly hope so, for both our sakes."

"Oh, I do, Mom. Really."

• • •

The motor running, warm for the first time in five whole days, I had to be careful not to fall asleep. I knew I shouldn't run the motor for longer than maybe half an hour, long enough to get warm and to charge the battery a little. I didn't know how long my exhaust hose would last, and I had to conserve on gas. I checked the gas gauge. A little more than five gallons. I had to dig myself out before I used up all the gas.

Unzipping my parka to feel the heat, I saw the radio. I'd been so crazy to get warm, I'd forgotten about the radio.

"Man, if it only worked. It would be so admirable, so worthy."

I turned the knob, heard the crackle, held my breath, breathed, whispered to myself, "Come on, come on," kept flipping stations.

All I got was music. I wanted to hear human voices. Then I got the ten o'clock local Silver City nightly news. The announcer reported some election or something, a fire, a robbery, and then: "As reported yesterday, the search for Kyle Hooper's body, the local boy lost in the avalanche in Silver Canyon, ended Tuesday evening after four days. Sheriff Catchwell's office further reports that the whole avalanche was covered without success. Kyle, an avid skier, was lost in the avalanche last Saturday when his Suburban was swept off the road. He was fifteen and a student at Jefferson High School. Kyle's family, all of whom are avid skiers, joined in the search, along with many of his high-school friends, neighbors, and members of his Mormon congregation. Authorities now say they'll have to wait until spring to recover the body. That could be late May or early June, depending of course on how warm the spring is. A memorial service is planned for after Christmas. The freeway was blocked today when a semi loaded with chickens tipped over . . ."

They'd stopped searching for me. I'd heard my name. I closed my eyes. Somehow I thought they all believed I was still alive. I didn't like them talking about my body like that, didn't want Lucille hearing what they said. I wanted them to still be searching for me and not waiting for the avalanche to melt. A memorial service was for when you didn't have a body, which was proof you were dead. They couldn't find Danny Fails's body when he drowned in the ocean on vacation to California with his family, so a memorial service is what they had, no casket or anything.

Lucille wouldn't let Trace just die. She nursed him night and day—checked his morphine drip because she was a nurse, gave him sponge baths, baked him his favorite desserts, sat up with him, did everything she could to make him better, until Dr. Wellmen said there wasn't any hope, and then Trace told her to let him die, although he didn't use that word.

"Mom, just let me go." Standing in our bedroom one evening, I heard Trace say that, his voice all whispery. "It'll be okay. I'm so tired, Mom. I hurt so bad. I'm not going to get better. I know that now. I had three blessings." Then he waited and said, "I saw Grandpa and Grandma Hooper. They were just standing there holding hands smiling. They're waiting for me, Mom. I'm not scared anymore."

"Oh, Trace, we all have dreams."

"It wasn't a dream, Mom. I was awake; it was night. They came two times, Mom. They know how sick I am."

Lucille sat on the edge of Trace's bed holding his hand and

kissing it and nodding her head and not saying anything, just crying, but not loud, the tears slipping down her cheeks.

"Oh, Trace. Oh, Trace. My wonderful son. My wonderful son."

"It's okay, Mom. I understand."

Lucille just kept nodding her head.

Three weeks before Trace died, I was in my bed lying there in the half darkness, my hands under my head, looking up at the white ceiling, when Trace said, his voice all whispery, "Kyle?" I'd thought he was asleep or drugged out because of the morphine.

I turned to face him. "Yeah."

"Be sure and take good care of my Martin."

"Oh, sure. I wish I could play it like you do."

And then Trace didn't say anything for a little while, and then he said, "I guess I should have learned to play the harp."

I didn't know what to say. I thought maybe I ought to laugh or maybe even say I was sorry, but I didn't. Trace didn't laugh or say anything else after that, just lay there quiet in the darkness. I didn't tell Lucille. I knew that Trace didn't want to die, didn't think that heaven, paradise, or whatever it was was better than good old Earth life. He just wanted to go on living his life, graduate from high school, go on a mission, go to college, maybe Stanford, play tennis, fall in love, get married, have kids, be some president of a big corporation or something, or maybe be this big singer.

I thought that was pretty portentous about Grandpa and Grandma Hooper showing up. I wish I'd seen them too, been awake, or they'd waked me up because I was in the same room with Trace. But I decided I wasn't supposed to. I was glad Grandpa Hooper was with Grandma Hooper and not stuck in some lower kingdom somewhere. He must have been more righteous than everybody thought, because he was always helping people. Grandma said Grandpa was the most generous person with his time that she'd ever met. I decided he probably had to quit swearing and drinking coffee. He never did smoke.

I sat forward in my seat looking at the radio.

"You think I'm dead, but I'm not. And stop talking about my dead body. And I don't want any grief counselors going to my classes either and telling my friends that everything is okay and they should all go on with their lives. I'm not dead. They shouldn't tell them that. It's not okay."

I knew that Lucille would have to go to school to empty my hall locker. And maybe it would be during class break, and Mark and some of the other guys would stop and tell Lucille what a great guy I was and how much they missed me.

"Thank you, boys. You're very kind. He was such a wonderful boy."

"We're really sorry, Mrs. Hooper."

And the guys would just stand there. Summer and other girls would stop too, just stand there looking so sad.

Lucille would probably say something religious like, "We'll all be together in the next life, won't we." Like she was trying to convert, because she was always doing that.

It was funny. Every day you saw a kid in the halls or in class, a kid you didn't really know but saw around, and then you heard he was dead. And kids talked about how he died and why, only sometimes it was a girl. And that was worse because girls weren't supposed to die or have anything bad happen to them. And you looked at the empty seat in class, if he was in your class, and you wondered what it felt like to die, right at the last minute, maybe even second, and if you knew you were dead and not alive any more.

And the grief counselor came to class, sometimes two of them, to convince you that dying was natural and nobody had to cry or get too upset if they only understood the circumstances, because high-school kids died too, not just old people, like that was supposed to cheer you up. Kids dying really only happened about once a year, maybe twice in the whole school, which is why they had this special page at the end of the yearbook for pictures of kids that died. Except if the kid had committed suicide, the grief counselors talked about asking for help if you were thinking about doing something like that, and nothing was so bad that you had to kill yourself.

And two or three days later you read the obituary and looked at the picture, which might be an old yearbook picture, which was the only picture the family had, the kid smiling and not dead. And if the obituary didn't say what the kid died of, or just said natural causes, you knew they probably OD'd or committed suicide or something.

I knew I should turn off the heater, but I just couldn't. It was so warm. Being warm was so beautiful, just beautiful.

Grandma and Grandpa Hooper's obituaries and Trace's, which Lucille wrote, listed all of their accomplishments, and what wonderful people they were, and how much they would be missed. It was like the obituary summed up their whole lives, and you couldn't be alive after your obituary was published in the *Herald*.

It surprised me that the *Herald* had an obituary page every day. I couldn't believe that so many people died in Silver City. Sometimes when I was looking for the sports page, I saw the obituary page. I looked at the pictures and read the names and birth and death dates, and most of them were old people. It usually said they were in the welcoming arms of Jesus, which I doubted because Jesus wouldn't have time to stand around with his arms out hugging everybody who died. He'd have other more important things to do like creating worlds or judging people and assigning them where they were supposed to go or something. The obituary always said how wonderful the person was, not saying they'd ever done anything wrong in their whole lives, which was kind of phony, but I guess it was okay, because the person was dead.

On Sundays there were always more obituaries than any other day, as if that were the best day for obituaries because people were thinking about heaven or something and all religious. And sometimes there was a picture of both the husband and the wife, only the wife wasn't dead, and she was there for support or something. But sometimes you just saw her hand on his shoulder, so you knew they'd cut the picture out of bigger one. Or there was a second picture of the dead person in high school, as if to prove they'd been young once, as if anybody doubted that. Sometimes even a picture of the person as a baby, which I thought must have been meant to prove the dead person had been born once or something, as if anybody doubted that either, because how could you die if you hadn't been born? And the *Herald* had pictures of Mormon missionaries too, mostly elders, who'd received their calls and where they were going, sometimes just across from the obituary page, the missionary looking all serious and religious, so you had to look twice to see he was still alive.

I wondered what Lucille would write about me. I hadn't earned my Eagle, wasn't a great athlete, not a straight-A student, didn't play the piano beautifully, wasn't a returned missionary (because I hadn't lived long enough obviously). I hadn't even been president of the deacons or the teachers quorum, just a counselor. Writing my obituary was going to be kind of tough on old Lucille.

Sitting there holding the quilt open to feel the awesome warmth, I still knew I was up only fifteen feet into the shaft, counting the cave. I'd spent all my time digging the tunnel and building the exhaust hose. I reached back to get the milk jug for a drink of pop.

"Oh, no." I almost swore, but I didn't.

The jug was empty. I'd accidentally tipped it over somehow. I hadn't found the lid, so I hadn't put it on. I'd have to drink water from Crystal Creek. I could tie a string to the bean can and dip it up. I might get some terrible disease, but that was okay.

"Stupid."

After having the heater on for half an hour, I put my boots back on, wrapped up in the warm quilt. I drank the rest of the catsup and poured the last gob of mayonnaise onto my hand and swallowed that. My stomach ached clear to my throat, I was so hungry. I'd rig the bean can and get a drink tomorrow. If I drank a lot of water I wouldn't feel so hungry, but I needed hot things to drink to build my core heat, not cold water. I could warm the water with the candle a little, but I needed to save the candle. The cold pop would have helped because of the sugar. I turned off the heater and then the light. Wrapped up in my quilt, I sniffed for carbon monoxide. It was so great to be warm again. I knew I would have died from hypothermia without the heater. I turned off the engine. I'd used over a gallon of gas already. I had to be careful.

Sixth Day, Thursday

I woke up shivering. Twice during the night I'd started the engine to get warm from the heater. If you died from hypothermia, they warmed your body up to be sure. The paramedics said you had to be warm and dead, not cold and dead. In deep hypothermia you sometimes breathed only two or three times a minute and had almost no pulse, so it was hard to tell if you were alive unless they got you warm and you started to breathe faster. You also automatically curled into the fetal position if you were dying. When I woke up, I always checked to see if I was fetal.

I turned on the light, started the engine, and waited for the heater to warm up, clenching my jaws and tightening my body against the shivering.

Later, sitting there, the heater going full blast, I thought about how great it was to go mountain biking on a hot summer day, wearing just shorts and shoes, the sun burning into you, feeling hot and sweaty. You gave it all you had, taking the steep trails, weaving around trees and boulders, making jumps, Mark right on your tail yelling and cheering, or you on his. Seeing the mountains, sheer cliffs, high peaks, the groves of aspen trees, alpine meadows as you tore by, you wanted just to keep going, feeling the thrill, sensing how good you were, taking chances, feeling everything, your mind shut off, not thinking.

Wishing Lucille didn't make you wear a helmet so you could feel your hair whipping back, your whole body feeling oiled, warm, you went faster and faster on the straightaways, like you wanted to do that the rest of your life. And then making the last jump, Mark making it too, slamming to a stop right beside you, throwing all this dust, laughing, pulling off his helmet.

"Awesome, Hooper. It's so awesome."

Our favorite run down out of Prospector Canyon went right by the juvenile detention center. The boys and girls divided, the boys walking around out in a chain-link fenced area or just standing talking to each other or shooting baskets. Or they stood facing the fence, arms reaching out, fingers stuck through the wire like they were trying to tear it down or like they were crucified or something.

Turning as you rode away, you saw this kid waving to you, and you waved back. He kept waving, and you wondered what he'd done to get himself incarcerated.

I'd always been afraid I'd end up in juvenile detention, but it wouldn't be my fault or anything. I'd have my license and probably be giving some kid a ride in the Suburban or something, when I'd hear a siren and look back and see about three cop cars behind me, or old Sheriff Catchwell probably if we were outside of town, red and blue lights flashing all over the place. And the kid would be a dealer, his pack full of about twenty pounds of weed or crack, or something. Catchwell would arrest us both for being dealers, and handcuff us, and impound my Suburban. And they'd fingerprint us and probably do a strip search, and wouldn't that be sweet? They'd take my belt and shoelaces so I wouldn't hang myself. How could a guy hang himself with shoelaces? And I'd get one phone call, just like in the flicks, and so I'd call Lucille because Frank would be out of town on one of his big deals probably. And I knew just what Lucille would say sitting across from me in the interrogation room.

"Well, Kyle, what's your excuse this time? This better be good."

"I didn't do anything, Mom. Just gave this kid named Stoner a ride after school. His pack was full of drugs. He's a dealer. Not me. I didn't know anything about it. What a loser. I'm innocent, Mom."

"Oh, I'm sure you are. Aren't you always? You'll be lucky if you don't end up in the state penitentiary. Of course, it will be a nice drive on Sunday afternoons for your father and me to come out and visit."

"Mom, you got to believe me."

"Oh, I do, but Sheriff Catchwell tells me you're going to have to spend the night in jail till we can get things straightened out, assuming that's possible."

"Mom, you can't let them do that to me."

"Afraid I can't do anything about it. Enjoy your stay, Kyle. Could be very educational. Your brother Nate had that same experience as I recall, or was that Clay? I'm sure it wasn't Trace."

"Please, Mom. I'll never get in trouble again. I promise."

"Isn't that what you said the last time? Sorry. Nothing I can do about it tonight. You'll have a hearing tomorrow. You're lucky you don't have to spend a week behind bars."

And so I'd have to spend the night in jail, probably with a bunch of drunks, druggies, and perverts, or something. And the next day Stoner would tell the cops that he was the dealer, not me, that I was just giving him a ride, and the cops would let me go and release my Suburban. And Lucille would tell me to follow her home, and when I got there, she'd say she was glad I didn't get ten years for dealing and possession, muss up my hair, give me a hug, and tell me there was a fresh chocolate cake on the counter if I wanted to invite Mark over.

"He's been over twice asking about you. You can tell him what it's like to be an arrested felon, be fingerprinted, strip-searched, and spend a night behind bars. He likes to hear about your adventures as I recall. You're quite an example, for a Mormon youth."

"Mom, please. It wasn't fun."

"Well, I'm certainly pleased to hear that. I thought maybe you might make a habit out of it. Not particularly commendable in a young man who holds the priesthood."

"Oh, brother."

When Lucille really gets anxious about my behavior, as she calls it, she always lays Moroni 9 from the Book of Mormon on me where the Nephites are all about to be killed off by the Lamanites in this big battle because the Nephites aren't spiritual anymore and delight in *abomination*, which is a word that has a different sort of sound. The Nephites are about as evil as you can get. They kill and torture people, rape young girls, even eat people, don't have any principles, and are past feeling. Lucille says that means you don't feel sorry for people or want to help them, or don't have any compassion or conscience or anything. You don't believe in the commandments or God or the Holy Ghost or anything, which sounds pretty evil I guess.

And I tell Lucille I'm not that bad.

"No," she says, "you're not. But it's something you need to think about."

"Oh, sure. I'm about to go off and start delighting in abomination."

"Well, from what I've heard, some of the kids at Jefferson High are experts."

"Yeah, sure, Mom."

• • •

With the Suburban heater still going full blast, I thought about working on the shaft all day. If I didn't run into any heavy spruce limbs or boulders, I could make two or three feet maybe. I'd be up to seventeen or eighteen. I might even break through. But I knew I was slowing down. It was funny to feel so weak and hungry, like my body couldn't move, especially my arms and legs, like I didn't have any muscles anymore, my whole body turned flabby. I couldn't shovel the snow into Crystal Creek anymore. I was too tired. I figured if I fainted or slipped and fell down the shaft, the piled icy snow would help break my fall. I knew I had to have a lot of faith or I was going to be sunk.

I put my feet up by the heater. I sniffed for exhaust fumes. I worried about my flashlight. The second set of batteries was already starting to get dim, and I knew the bulb might burn out. I still had the candle and the last set of batteries, but that would be it.

I looked at my phone on the dash. Everything could have been so simple. The gas was down to four gallons.

"Always work smart, Kyle," Grandpa Hooper always said. "Hell, no point in worrying about what might have been. Life's too short. Don't do things half-assed either. Use your head. That's what it's for."

When I'd looked down at Grandpa Hooper in his casket at the funeral home, I was surprised he didn't have a sucker in his mouth.

In world history we'd studied all about what good embalmers the Egyptians were and how they buried things with you that you were going to need in the next life. The American Indians did that too, even a warrior's horse, which they had to kill first of course. I thought that was a pretty good idea. I had a few things I'd like to take with me, like my sharp clothes, all my DVDs, phone, iPod, a TV, a computer, and my mountain bike, my skis. Grandpa Hooper told me once about one of his friends who was buried in this old convertible Cadillac he loved so much and drove for twenty years. It took six burial plots.

"Do they ski in heaven? Can you drive an old Suburban around? Can you date girls? What's the food like? Do you get to sleep or are you awake all the time? Can you go swimming, run cross-country, go mountain biking? What is there to do anyway? Do you still have to work on being all perfect? How do you build all these kingdoms?" I asked these questions just to hear my voice, but I also wanted to know. What was there to do? Why even go if you just sat around or spent most of your time singing in heavenly choirs? I asked Lucille that one day when she was proving difficult about my B- in seminary, just to show her how interested I was in religion.

"Oh, ye of little faith," she said.

"Mom, I was just asking."

"Never mind. Never mind. If you don't know at least a little by now about the kingdoms and glories, eternal families, living with God and his Son Jesus Christ, the Millennium, and eternal progress, I couldn't explain it to you if I had all day."

"Try me. Sounds really mellifluous."

"Don't you get smart with me, young man. Go finish practicing the piano. You may have put in all of fifteen minutes earlier."

"Mom."

"What, dear?"

"Nothing. Nothing at all."

• • •

I put my arms around my stomach and pulled in tight against the ache. I wasn't starving yet, but I was getting weaker. Turning in the seat, I looked to see if I'd missed anything edible maybe. I reached over and picked up an orange peel. I'd dropped all the peelings on the back seat and on the floor. I ate it, and then got up and gathered all the peelings I could find and stuffed them into my pockets. I'd eat them while I was working on the shaft. I picked up all the banana peelings. They wouldn't be as good as orange peelings, but they'd help. I cut them up into little pieces so I could suck on them. I chewed on a mouthful of orange peelings, swallowing the juice and then the warm pulp, feeling it go down.

I knew I should turn off the engine and get to work, but I didn't want to stop being warm.

Sitting there, I made a mental list of all the kinds of food I liked—hamburgers, steaks, roasts, potatoes and gravy, apple pie, chocolate cake, oatmeal-raisin cookies, waffles, French bread, fresh peaches and cream, chocolate shakes, strawberries and cream, hot-fudge sundaes with nuts and real whipped cream like Lucille makes, not that canned stuff. I really liked to eat. There was always something good to eat in the fridge for me and Mark. Lucille was a great cook but was always telling me not to eat too much.

"You'd better slow down on the pie and cake, Romeo, or the girls won't be attracted to that body you're so proud of—those steel-like abs, sinewy arms and legs, that chiseled chin. Girls notice things like that."

"Mom, why can't you be serious?"

"Oh, I am."

Sometimes I lifted weights in front of the mirror just to see my muscle definition. I liked being buff. One of the reasons I didn't do drugs was because of my body, what drugs could do to me, make my teeth fall out, my brain turn to mush, my muscles go all flabby. How could you fry your brain so you couldn't think about anything, just sit around staring at the wall drooling? It would be so detrimental. Kids at school stole money from their parents, took things from the house to hawk, robbed people at night, broke into stores, dealt, did anything just to have money for drugs, like taking drugs was the most important thing in their whole lives, and they couldn't stop even if they wanted to. I knew two priests from the ward, Highman and Potter, who went all deviant once they got turned on to drugs, which nobody knew about of course, not even their families. They both blessed the sacrament one Sunday morning and were in the slammer, which is what Grandpa Hooper called jail, that afternoon for dealing. Sometimes Grandpa also called it the clink or the hoosegow. I liked all three words.

Thinking about food, swallowing hard, chewing another mouthful of orange peelings, I reached over and turned off the engine. I had to get back to work digging. Glancing down, I saw on the dash where I'd marked the days. It was the sixth day. I wiped the melting frost off the rearview mirror to look at my thin, dark face. I touched my face. Except where my goggles fit, it was almost black from the dirt. I looked at my fingers.

One of the first climbers to ever climb Everest had to have all his frostbitten fingers and toes cut off, but he said it didn't matter; it was worth it because he'd climbed Everest. I tried to imagine what it would be like.

"Hey, man, how could you eat, shake hands with people, operate a computer, dress yourself, go to the bathroom, drive a car, or make love when you're married? How do you walk without toes, or run, or ski?" I wanted to ask him that. "Do you just sit there all day looking at your stumpy hands and feet and think about how wonderful climbing Everest was? What about all the guys who climbed it and didn't lose their fingers and toes, some of them living till they were ninety?"

Not me. After my mission I was going to go to college, really study hard, and date all these really classy girls, party a lot, just enjoy myself, get a great job, buy me a car, have my own apartment, go on skiing trips to Switzerland. And then I'd get married when I was about twenty-five, maybe twenty-seven, maybe even thirty, and get really serious about life like Lucille was always telling Nate and Clay.

• • •

Outside the Suburban, I punched a hole in the rim of the bean can, tied a piece of string to it, and got a drink from Crystal Creek. I needed to drink a gallon of hot chocolate to get warm. But I didn't have any mix or a stove to heat it on. Standing on the logs over the creek, I spit, but it still didn't freeze or crackle.

When I went fishing with Grandpa Hooper, we used to drink from a spring in the big grove of spruce trees. You didn't have to worry about giardia drinking from a spring.

The mink still hadn't eaten the beans.

"Where are you, mink? I guess you don't like beans, just fish?"

I reached down and picked up the three frozen beans and put them in my mouth. I didn't chew them, just let them melt and sucked on them so they'd last.

I climbed up into the shaft. I went to put the flashlight in the hole, but dropped it. "No! No!" I looked down. It was still lit. "Oh, thank you. Thank you." Going down the shaft in the half-dark I was really scared, feeling for each foothold with my heavy ski boots. If I fell and broke my leg, or maybe both legs, I knew I'd just lie there in the pile of snow and die a terrible, slow, lingering death.

Lucille was always warning me about being careful when I was mountain biking, skate boarding, diving off cliffs into the Silver River, or skiing and doing all these great jumps with Mark and the other guys. She'd tell stories about kids who were paralyzed because they broke their backs. She was big on fractured skulls, broken necks, and broken backs.

"Boys who break their backs or necks have a particularly difficult life, Kyle, assuming they live of course. They can't get up to go to the bathroom. They have to have a catheter for urine and have the pleasure of wearing diapers again. And it's questionable that they will ever be fathers."

"Mom, I'm not going to break anything. I'm not that dumb."

"Well, it's been known to happen. Just thought I'd mention it."

I could see old Sheriff Catchwell and a couple of deputies sliding me into one of those black body bags with a zipper like a sleeping bag, those bags they're always dragging out on TV cop shows. They always show the autopsy room too, the corpse under a sheet on a stainless-steel table. They sometimes show the top half if it's a man or just to her neck if it's a woman, with a name tag tied to one of the big toes. But you know you'd be completely naked just lying there. They bag you and put you in a big drawer, the whole wall lined with drawers on rollers, a body in each one, like the narrow sock drawer in your bedroom dresser.

And Lucille would have to identify me, and they'd pull open the drawer with me in it and unzip the bag so Lucille could see my face. And she'd nod just like they do on TV, not say anything, be all silent because it was so tragic. Nate, Clay, Brooke, and Jed would be there standing by her, and they'd nod too, but not Frank because of course he'd be in Chicago or someplace on some big deal. Brooke would have her arm around Lucille, tears streaming down Lucille's face, and they'd all just stand there because it would be so incomprehensible that I could have perished, because I was such a great kid.

Before Trace died he got so weak and had to use a commode and then a bed pan. He sometimes asked me to help him to the bathroom. I held his thin arm so he could walk, helped him get his pajama pants down, and kind of lowered him onto the toilet.

"Thanks, Kyle." Trace said that every time I helped him; he'd stopped calling me kid. I never thought he would ever have to thank me for something like that, be so humble. I wasn't embarrassed helping him. He was sick. It was different.

I also helped Trace get into the shower and reached in and held his arm so he didn't fall. He was so thin, his bones pushing tight against his pale skin. I helped Trace get into his clean pajamas and even combed his hair for him. He looked different, like being sick made him look older. I liked being able to help him; I liked that he wanted me to help, like I was growing up or something. I never thought I'd ever have to help him like I did. Combing his hair seemed the most personal thing to do for him. His hair was longer. It was like his head was shrinking or something, his white skin tight and shiny against his skull.

"It's nice to be clean again, Kyle. Thanks." That was before he got so weak and Lucille started giving him sponge baths, which I knew I didn't ever want Lucille to have to give me ever, even if she was a nurse.

At night, the lights out, Trace, his voice whispery in the shadowy half-darkness, asked me about school and my classes, but sometimes he didn't ask any questions, just lay there, and I thought he might be dead. And I'd go over and close his eyes like they do in the flicks and then go tell Lucille and Frank, if he was home. I'd stopped working out with my weights because it didn't seem right for Trace to have to watch me, but Trace told me to go ahead, and he watched. He was six-one, on the varsity tennis team even as a freshman. He was always playing his Martin and singing at parties and on school talent shows and things. Lucille was always saying "Hey, handsome" to Trace, or maybe dream boat or good-looking, and stuff like that. She never said that to me. She called me cute, which was okay. It didn't bother me.

• • •

Standing there at the bottom of the shaft holding the flashlight, I was so tired, cold, and hungry. I'd eaten all the orange peelings. I started eating the banana peelings, sucking on them so they kind of melted. They were hard to chew. I

thought about eating the candle, but I knew I'd need it when
the flashlight went out.

After I climbed back up, I got the candle and some matches
out of the toolbox, wrapped them in a piece of aluminum
foil to keep them dry, and put them in the zippered inside
pocket of my parka. I wasn't going to make that same dumb
mistake again and be without light in the shaft if I dropped the
flashlight or it went out. I knew I couldn't keep making dumb
mistakes. Just simple little mistakes got you killed. I had to
keep thinking.

My freshman year, two seniors, Bob Klinker and Eric
Motely, got drunk, and Eric, who was driving, rolled his Jeep
out four-wheeling at two in the morning and Bob got killed.
Eric's kid brother Wayne told me and Mark and the other guys
all about it, shaking his head all the time because it was so bad,
us standing there listening.

"They didn't wear seat belts, and when Eric came to he
crawled over by Bob. He kept telling Bob not to die, but he
was choking, blood coming out of his mouth and nose, so he
died anyway. And Eric right there with him, holding his head
on his lap. And Eric phoned Dad and asked what he should
do. That night Mom and Dad took Eric over to tell Bob's folks
how sorry he was. Dad said he had to go to Bob's funeral too.
At the viewing Bob was right there in the casket dressed in
a suit and a white shirt and tie, not even looking hurt. His
girlfriend Sylvie Sadly stood there crying. Eric cried all the
time too. And Bob's mom put her arms around him and told
him again they didn't blame him because Bob could have been
driving and they were best friends. All the football coaches
and the whole team came to the funeral because they were
both starters. All the pallbearers were on the team, and they all
wore their helmets, which looked kind of funny, these six guys
in suits and ties and wearing football helmets, but at least they
didn't wear their whole uniforms with cleats and everything.

Eric had to go to court for drunk driving, but they didn't put him in jail." Wayne just stood there shaking his head. "It was so awful."

"Yeah."

I'd been a pallbearer for Trace but not for Grandpa Hooper because I was too young; just my three brothers were. It felt strange holding onto the casket handle, lifting, feeling the weight, and knowing Trace's body was inside. Nate, Clay, me, and three cousins were pallbearers. We all wore white carnations in our lapels; at the cemetery we took them off and placed them on top of Trace's casket that hung on wide straps over the open grave, and you were careful because you might slip and fall in. You couldn't see any dirt; they'd draped artificial grass down into the grave to the cement vault so it wasn't like Trace was being buried in dirt. Off to the side, I saw the big cement lid that went on the vault. I saw Lucille sitting on the front row of folding canvas chairs under the green canopy, shaking her head, wiping her eyes with Frank's big white handkerchief, Frank's arm around her.

• • •

Standing there by the shaft, when I turned to climb up I saw the mink on a log. It looked at me and then slipped down between two logs and was gone. I was glad to see the mink. It was important somehow.

Digging, I ran into a tangle of spruce limbs all about five inches in diameter. I cut through them with the bow saw, but it took hours, and I was too tired, weak, and cold to work any longer. I didn't know how much longer I could keep going. I hoped I didn't hit the trunk of a big ninety-foot spruce. I'd never be able to cut through it.

Later, sitting in the Suburban, the ceiling light on, I started the engine. I kept sniffing for exhaust fumes. I was down to three gallons of gas. I had to dig my way out before the gas was gone. I had to have heat and light.

I'd eaten my last piece of banana peeling hours ago. I knew I was starving. I was so weak. I had to have something to eat. If only I could fry the two pounds of hamburger I'd tossed in the back. That was all I had left. I knew that in Japan they ate raw fish, so raw hamburger couldn't be that bad, could it? It was just raw cow, wasn't it? Sitting there, I knew right where the hamburger was in the back of the Suburban in the snow. I pushed the quilt back and went and got it. Standing by the door of the Suburban, I held it against the heater until I could take off the plastic wrapping. It was frozen solid. I got the hammer out of the toolbox, went outside, put the hamburger on the hard snow, and hit it. It broke in two pieces. I hit it four more times. It was all in small pieces.

I picked up a piece. I looked at it. I brushed it off on my parka. I put it in my mouth. I held it in the front of my mouth. I couldn't taste anything. I tried not to touch it with my tongue. It got soft, and I swallowed it. I didn't need to chew it. I waited. I didn't throw up. I hadn't tasted anything. I put four more pieces in my mouth one at a time and swallowed them when they got soft. I wrapped the other pieces in the plastic and took them inside the Suburban and buried them in the snow. I wanted them to stay good and frozen. I knew I could eat the hamburger if it stayed frozen. It wasn't that bad. On their missions Nate and Clay had to eat all kinds of strange things in Russia and Peru, things they didn't know the names of. They sometimes had to fast and pray for two whole days for investigators so they would get a testimony and join the Church. It would take a lot of faith.

My boots off, wrapped in the quilt, I sat in the Suburban getting warm. It was like my whole body had to thaw out now, not just my hands and feet. My gloves were pulling apart along the seams. My body was getting stiffer, heavier, and harder to move. I knew that I'd probably already be dead if I didn't have the heater. I thought about what it would be like to die if you were conscious, which Trace wasn't. You'd just sense yourself slowly dying, everything getting blurry, the feeling starting to go out of your hands and feet. But I didn't like thinking about that. I crawled to the back and got three more pieces of hamburger. I knew if I ate too much I might get sick. But I was still hungry.

I had the radio turned on to the ten o'clock news. The announcer talked about a robbery, a fire, and an auto-pedestrian accident. He didn't say anything about me; I knew he wouldn't. I knew I wouldn't be on the TV news either. They thought I was toast. I wondered if Lucille had started writing my obituary yet. I knew she wouldn't want to. Brooke had helped her write Trace's, Lucille wiping the tears away with her white handkerchief all the time, saying, "I just can't believe that wonderful boy is gone. I just can't believe it."

I knew they'd have to do an autopsy on me when they found me, because it would be an unattended death. Billy Whimly had asked the paramedics if they had to do that if you froze to death.

"Well, that depends on whether you're alone or somebody's with you and sees you die. If nobody is, then that's an unattended death. You might have been murdered or committed suicide or something, so they have to check that out."

"What if you're still alive when they do it? You're just in a coma or something and not really dead yet and they can't really tell?"

"Well, I suppose that could have happened a hundred years ago, but they're a lot more careful than they used to be. Maybe it could happen when there's a train wreck or an earthquake or something and there's hundreds of dead people so you're rushed bagging bodies."

I knew that when they did an autopsy on a cop show they

cut up through your ribs with an electric saw. You didn't actually see them do it, but there'd be this doctor or somebody in a white apron holding the saw, and you knew that's what they were doing, which was pretty egregious. And they cut off the top of your skull and took out your brain and weighed it, and they weighed your liver and kidneys too, although I didn't know why, and that was gross too. I'd heard stories of a live person on the autopsy table who was able just at the last moment to blink or move his little finger. And the doctor noticed it out of the corner of his eye, turned off the saw, and they revived this guy, and didn't do the autopsy. That would be so horrendous to see some guy in a white apron coming at you with an electric saw or a big pair of scissors. I'd thought about that happening to me.

I'd probably be driving the Suburban over to some lovely's house and get T-boned by a semi that ran a stop light, and suffer a terrible head injury and be in a deep coma so the paramedics probably wouldn't check very closely because I was obviously dead with this big hole in my head and blood all over. And Frank and Lucille and my whole family would be home crying when the doctors were doing the autopsy, but I'd wake up just when they had me on the stainless-steel table all naked under the sheet with a tag tied on my big toe. I couldn't move or talk, but one tear would slip down my cheek from one eye because I'd be so sad. And the doctor would yell and drop the electric saw, so they wouldn't have to do the autopsy. And they'd call my family, who would be so happy and come rushing back to the hospital because I was alive and not dead. And I'd recover completely, even with the big hole in my head.

But when I was healed and everything, Lucille would tell me I had to learn to drive defensively, which she was always telling me, and make me take another defensive-driving course.

I'd look at Lucille. "Mom, the guy in the semi ran the light, not me. He T-boned me. I was almost dead."

"I know, but if you'd been watching instead of daydreaming about some girl, you would have seen it coming. Semi trucks are fairly easy to see in broad daylight in Silver City. You should have counted one, two, three, four, five before starting through a green light, like I taught you, and you wouldn't have been hit. You never know if a driver is going to stop on a red light."

"Yeah, sure. I should have counted to a million. I'd still be there."

"Don't you get smart with me, young man."

"Oh, the thought never crossed my mind."

"Kyle."

Whenever some kid OD'd, got drunk out of his mind, annihilated himself and about six other people in a head-on going ninety out on the freeway, or splashed his brains on a tree skiing downhill out of control, Lucille always read me the newspaper article at supper. Even if the kid lived in some town three hundred miles away, or in another state even. We'd be eating supper, probably fried chicken, which I really like, with apple pie and ice cream for dessert, which I also like, and then she'd hand me the paper so I wouldn't miss the pictures, just to remind me what could happen to me.

"Okay, Mom. I get the message. I'll be careful."

"Very reassuring, Kyle."

"I really will, Mom. Just no more newspaper articles for a while, okay? I'd like to enjoy supper. I've had a long day."

"Oh, I'm sure you have, Kyle, all that studying you do. What was your grade point last term, 4.0?"

"It was a bad term."

"Oh, I'm sure it was."

I got a 3.0, which wasn't bad, except for seminary, where old Glimmer gave me a B- just because I hadn't memorized at least half the Book of Mormon. But your seminary grade wasn't counted in your GPA, so that wasn't that big a catastrophe. I knew I could get into State with a 3.0. Then I really planned to study, be an engineer, a doctor, or something, make all this money so I could enjoy life.

• • •

Wrapped in my quilt, leaning back in the seat, all I wanted to do was sleep. I had to be careful. It was so easy just to drift off to sleep with the motor running. My hose could break anytime and fill the Suburban with carbon monoxide.

Lucille was tough, but she was okay. You just had to know how to take her. She'd almost made herself sick trying to make Trace better. Dr. Wellmen told her she would get seriously ill and be headed to the hospital or worse herself if she didn't get some rest.

"That doesn't matter," she said in the hall talking to Wellmen. "All that matters is Trace."

"Yes, I understand that, Lucille, but Trace isn't going to get better. You know that and I know that. I thought you'd accepted that fact. You've taken him to three specialists. They all say the same thing. You need to take care."

"Perhaps."

Trace's clothes hung in the closet after he died; and then one day they were gone, his two dresser drawers empty. Lucille had given them all to Good Will. She'd asked me if I wanted any of Trace's clothes, and I said no. She did what she had to do. She left all his photos on the cork board.

I didn't want Lucille to have to do that for me, folding my T-shirts and shorts, my jeans, putting my socks in a bag, and then taking all my sharp shirts, pants, sweaters, ties, and three sport coats out of the closet, giving everything to Good Will. And some mother would buy them for her son, they were so sharp. I didn't think Good Will took socks, T-shirts, or shorts; what would that feel like wearing some dead guy's stuff against your skin?

I could just see Lucille driving up to Good Will. When the lady opened the boxes, she'd say, "These really are nice things. Some young man will be very happy to get them. Did your son outgrow everything? Boys do grow so fast, don't they?"

"Yes they do." That's all Lucille would say. She wouldn't explain I'd been killed in an avalanche. She'd just walk out the door.

I started thinking about all the nice things Lucille was always doing for me—typing my English papers, slipping me ten bucks for no reason, buying me a really classy tie I didn't need, doing my laundry when I let it pile up, making my favorite dessert, taking me wherever I needed to go, and letting me drive after I got my learner's permit. So I had to sort of go along, so she knew I understood and was grateful, sort of anyway. But of course she'd sit right beside me in the car telling me what I was doing wrong and to watch every car on the road, even if it was half a mile away and going twenty miles an hour. Lucille was actually okay most of the time, but you really had to be patient with her.

She even taught me how to dance, and she did that for my brothers too. She said, "Girls don't actually like to have their feet stepped on, Kyle, although that may come as a surprise. You'd think they were dancing with a buffalo. What some girls have to put up with just to get a date. It's a crime. Dance all night with some oaf who doesn't know his right foot from his left and thinks the girl is highly privileged because he asked her for a date. It makes you wonder why all these girls don't become nuns."

It was kind of funny at first dancing with Lucille, her head on my shoulder, smelling her hair, but then it was okay. And it was surprising how many girls liked to waltz. They thought it was very romantic, which was all right with me. Lucille said that girls liked to be held but it wasn't necessary to break any ribs. Trace was the best dancer out of all four of us boys, of course. Sometimes in the evening Lucille put on music and she and Trace would dance in the family room, very smooth, which she'd do with me too but not as often as with Trace.

I really wanted a steady girlfriend like Summer, just to be mine and nobody else's. I'd give her Christmas and birthday presents, and she'd give me presents, and I'd take her to all the dances, games, and parties. She'd always smile when she saw me in the hall and leave her girlfriends and come over to me. And we'd take most of our classes together and sit across from each other to text and hold hands when old Tolson or some other teacher wasn't looking. And all the other guys would know she was my girlfriend and not try to hang out with her. That would be so copacetic, so worthy. But of course that's just what Lucille was all against until after my mission, like I didn't have any self-control or anything and had to date all these different girls like some kind of marathon or something. What fun would that be? You wouldn't even be able to kiss them good night, if you only dated them once, probably. But of course I'd have to bring every girl by the house so Lucille could check her out, which is what she did with my brothers, even perfect Trace; and Brooke had to bring her boyfriends by too for inspection.

It wasn't just kissing and holding hands either. Mostly I wanted a girl as a friend. Mark was a great buddy, but I wanted a girlfriend too. Girls are different, the way they walk, look at you, smile, even laugh, and what it feels like when you hold hands. It wasn't anything about sex, really. I'd grown up knowing about sex. I can't remember when I didn't know about sex. It was just something I knew, Lucille telling me things I needed to know when I was old enough because sex wasn't some big mystery, which was embarrassing kind of, but not that bad, sort of interesting. Like at first Lucille would sit next to me at the kitchen table and have me look up words about sex in the dictionary and pronounce them and read the definitions. She'd gone with me to the maturation lecture in the sixth grade, but she said that wasn't nearly as detailed as it should be, and not nearly early enough either.

"Okay, you can pronounce that word at least. Now read the definition out loud." I read it. "Good, now do you understand what that word means, Kyle?"

"I guess."

"What do you mean, you guess? Do you understand it or not? I don't want some older boys filling your head with a lot of nonsense about your sexual development. Sex is perfectly normal and beautiful."

"Oh, sure. It couldn't be clearer."

"Don't get smart with me, young man."

"Mom, please. I can't stand anymore."

"I just want to be sure you understand."

"Oh, I understand. Please, Mom."

When I was twelve Lucille brought out her old nursing biology text to show me drawings about human reproduction, had me read two sex pamphlets, *Sex and the Pubescent Boy* and *Questions a Boy Should Ask His Mom and Dad About Sex*. And then when I was fourteen she'd shown me her STD video. I didn't ask Lucille about sex; she just told me, just like she told my brothers and Brooke, so we all knew about it, showed them the video too. I got so I wasn't even curious about sex, but just about girls really. There's a big difference. My friends, even Mark a little bit, had such strange ideas about sex, had all these crazy stories about what people did, so I had to explain things to them and straighten them out. Sex was just sex, like breathing, just perfectly normal, except of course you had to be back from your mission and married first.

Seventh Day, Friday

I woke up. I felt light-headed, a little spacey. After I turned on the light and warmed up the engine, I turned on the heater. When I was warm, I pulled off my quilt and got some more pieces of frozen hamburger. I cut open the plastic catsup and mayonnaise bottles lengthways so I could lick up all that was left, and that helped the slick hamburger taste better. I still kept worrying there might have been another big snowstorm or another avalanche had come down on the first one. But God had to be fair, didn't he? He hadn't let the exhaust pipe or the muffler get broken. I just knew I had to keep digging because that was all I could do, and keep having faith.

Sitting there, I kept imagining what it would be like getting out of the avalanche after everybody thought I'd been dead for six days. If it was evening and nobody saw me climbing out of the shaft, I'd hitch a ride home and just walk right into the house. I wouldn't stop at the lodge and phone or anything or tell the ski patrol. Lucille would throw some kind of a fit.

"Kyle! Kyle! Kyle!" she'd scream and throw her arms around me and hug me and pull back and run her hand through my hair like she always did, Sadie barking and jumping up on me. "Oh, Kyle. Thank God, thank God you're safe, you're alive. You're not hurt or anything?"

"I'm fine, Mom, just fine."

"You're fine, are you? *Just fine?*"

And then she'd tear into me for taking the Suburban and getting caught in the avalanche and worrying them all to death. And then she'd hug me again and say it didn't matter because I was home safe and start hugging me again, and ask me all kinds of questions, and probably want to take me to the hospital, I'd look so beat. She'd call the whole family, even my cousins, uncles, and aunts, and Mark and Bishop Goodmer and President Smyles to come to the house to have a prayer. And Frank would give me a big hug and say how grateful they all were to have me back alive.

I'd tell her I'd learned my lesson and how grateful I was for everything, and I was going to help her with the outside Christmas lights, vacuum the whole house, empty the dishwasher, do my own laundry, practice the piano at least two hours a day, including Saturday and Sunday, and do anything else she wanted me to. Get up early to go to seminary and not complain, go on a mission. I'd had plenty of experience smoothing down her ruffled feathers. But I knew I'd really change too because of all I'd suffered and how scared I'd been of dying.

Lucille would fix me this big meal with all my favorite foods, including thick slices of roast beef with lots of mashed potatoes and gravy, about a quarter of an apple pie with vanilla ice cream, crying all the time and saying how grateful she was and her prayers had been answered. And I'd shower for about a month, draining both tanks, but Lucille wouldn't care she'd be so happy. Dressed in clean clothes but not wearing shoes, just socks, I'd wrap up in a blanket and lie in front of the fireplace with a big fire going, Sadie next to me. It would be so great to be warm and clean again and not hungry, just sort of grateful for the Holy Ghost, who really worked when you needed him.

I'd call up Mark and my other buddies, and they wouldn't believe it was me. Maybe I wouldn't call Mark, just walk in on him, not ring the doorbell, just like I always did.

"Hey, man, I thought you were dead. What a phony. Can't you do anything right, Hooper?"

And then Mark would shake my hand, probably give me a hug he would be so excited, laughing all the time, wiping the tears out of his eyes with the back of his hand. And Mark's mom would hug and kiss me and probably cry.

Going to school the next day would be a riot. Tolson would probably pass out when I walked into class, all the boys clapping and yelling and giving me high fives, the girls smiling, their eyes wet with tears they were so grateful. The TV people might even come to school to interview me.

We'd read *Tom Sawyer* in English in the eighth grade. I really liked the part where Tom and Huck, who were supposed to be drowned in the Mississippi River, showed up at their own funeral. That was so worthy. Maybe if I didn't dig myself out for a whole week or maybe longer, they'd be having my funeral, or maybe just a memorial service because they didn't have a body of course. And I'd just open the big double doors of the church and walk in. And the speaker, maybe my track coach or somebody, would just stop, stand there at the pulpit staring at me, and then everybody would turn to look at me. I'd be all dirty and thin because I was starving, my eyes sunken in, with dried blood down the side of my face from getting hit by the can of pork and beans. I'd probably be staggering just a little because of all I'd suffered, and then somebody would shout, "He's alive! Look, Kyle's alive!" And the whole ward would start shouting and cheering, some old sisters passing out probably, and my whole family would come rushing down the aisle to hug and kiss me. And Bishop Goodmer would say they'd just have a closing hymn and a prayer of gratitude and dismiss the meeting because it was a miracle and everybody would be too excited to hear the speakers, who'd be pretty boring anyway of course.

• • •

I worked for almost an hour until I got dizzy in the shaft, but when I climbed down out I felt better. So I knew I probably wasn't getting enough oxygen in the shaft, or I was using it all up or something. But there was nothing I could do about that. I didn't have any way of rigging an exhaust fan. I just had to climb down and fill my lungs with fresh air. The flashlight went out, and I had to climb down in the dark and put in the last set of batteries.

I'd begun to feel like a mole. The fish and salamanders in pools of water in caves didn't have eyes because they didn't need them. Being in the dark alone was a bad feeling. I wasn't afraid of the dark, but it bothered me to think that if I didn't dig my way out, when the gas, batteries, and candle were gone, I wouldn't even have the dash light. The only thing I could do then was feel around with my hands to know where I was and what I was doing. And I'd just have to sit in the Suburban wrapped in my quilt and slowly die of hypothermia or just freeze to death, first my hands and feet and then my arms and legs turning numb, my eyes turning icy, till I eventually perished.

Later in the Suburban, resting and getting warm because I couldn't work any longer, I saw the scratches I'd made on the dash for each day. I added them up. It was December twenty-second. I'd been under the avalanche for seven days. January twenty-third was my birthday. I'd be sixteen in a month. I sat there. I couldn't believe it.

"I'll be sixteen." I said that quietly to myself. There was something wonderful, almost magical, about being sixteen. It meant you weren't a kid anymore; I wasn't sure what, but something more important, like you were almost grown up and could do whatever you wanted and nobody could stop you, and you could get your driver's license and be able to drive all by yourself wherever you wanted to and go on dates all alone by yourself just with a girl. The first thing I was going to do was take Summer Landers on a date. I wasn't going to double-date with Mark, not this first time; I just wanted to be with Summer alone and really talk to her.

But I knew you had to watch it. Coming out of seminary two weeks ago after Brother Glimmer had given his big annual lesson on staying clean and pure, I was right behind Sill Synner and Jere Wantin when Sill said to Jere, "How are you this morning, Miss Clean and Pure?"

"Wonderful. And how are you, Mr. Clean and Pure?"

"Oh, wonderful too."

And then they stopped for this big kiss right there in the middle of the sidewalk, real voluptuaries. Everybody at school knew they were sleeping together, but still they went to seminary and church. I guess nobody in their wards knew, including their parents.

Being sixteen you had to think about things more, who you were and what you wanted, and what was important and what wasn't. Your dad ordaining you a priest and you blessing the sacrament in front of everybody in church, not just passing it, and not making a mistake in the prayer and having to do it over. What you were going to do all your life was important because you couldn't just stay sixteen, although maybe that's what you wanted to do. People expected you to do things, like graduate from high school, go on a mission, go to college, get a good job, get married, buy a house, have kids, stay active in the Church, have all this faith, become really spiritual, and be a bishop or stake president maybe eventually, maybe even an apostle if you were righteous enough, which was a lot of extra work. Things could really get complicated.

"You know you're fertile, don't you?" Lucille had asked me that when I was fourteen, and she was talking to me about how to treat my dates with respect after I turned sixteen.

"Fertile?"

"Yes, fertile. It means you could get some girl pregnant, if you felt inclined. You know that?"

"Well, sure, I guess."

"What do you mean by you guess? Either you know it or you don't. Either you can or you can't."

"Well, it's not something I think about every day."

"Well, you'd better think about it. Your older brothers have managed so far not to bring girlfriends home with the happy news that your father and I are going to be grandparents. We'd like you to follow their sterling example, if you're so inclined."

"Sure, Mom."

"Well, thank you. We appreciate your willingness to cooperate. There's half an apple pie in the fridge if you're interested, unless of course you and Mark have already devoured it."

When I told Mark what Lucille had said about my being fertile, he couldn't stop laughing.

"Hey, we're fertile. Lucille is so awesome."

"Yeah, tell me all about it."

For about a week after that, every time Mark saw me, he'd say, "Hey, Fertile, how's it going?"

Lucille also straightened me out on the word *special,* which they were always hitting us youth with in church, telling us how special we were, or that we were a chosen generation.

"Well, I wouldn't worry too much about being special, young man. Just try to be decent. They feed you kids that special stuff so much you actually begin to believe it. It breeds arrogance. Mormon kids begin to think they're better than everybody else just because they happen to be members of the true church. Just try for a little humility before you worry too much about how special you are. There are plenty of decent kids at Jefferson High who aren't Mormon, Mark and Chris for example. And as far as being a chosen generation, they were telling us that when I was a kid, and my mother before that, so don't worry too much about how special you are. You know what humility means, don't you, Kyle?"

"Oh, sure."

• • •

Opening the quilt to let the heat in, I thought about how sad it was going to be if I didn't get to be sixteen. It would be so sad. I closed my eyes and clenched my jaws, it would be so sad.

"Man. Man. Really sad. You just got to be sixteen."

Mark's mom had thrown a big party for him when he turned sixteen, and Lucille was planning one for me and all my friends with all kinds of great food. She was even going to let me skip a couple of classes so I could go down to get my driver's license. She said she and Frank were going to give me some big present. I didn't know what it was, but I knew it was something really great because it was my sixteenth birthday. Maybe a TV for my room, if she was really magnanimous, which was something I really wanted. But Lucille had already put the skids under that.

"You watch enough TV, Kyle. You would spend half your life watching TV and playing video games if I let you. No point in encouraging you."

"Ah, Mom. It'd be so great just to lie in bed and have my own TV."

"I'm sure it would be, Kyle. Forget about it."

I was arguing with her once about having a TV, and she said she was glad I wasn't an accident because that would be too much to take. I said, "Not an accident?"

"Yes. You were wanted. Your conception was intended. Do you understand? Some conceptions aren't intended. People call them accidents."

"Oh."

"Oh? Is that all you can say?"

"I guess."

"You guess?" Lucille shook her head. "Why bother to explain anything? Go finish ironing your shirts."

I thought about that, Frank and Lucille deciding to have another baby on purpose and then having me, although they didn't know whether I would be a boy or a girl or what kind of person I would be. But they had to take what they got. It was interesting to think about. Maybe I was a super spirit or something just waiting with all those other spirits in the preexistence for a chance to be born. Or maybe God, or whoever was responsible for that kind of thing, had assigned me to the Hooper family. I hadn't thought about that before, being assigned because God knew I was such a diligent spirit, or something, maybe even like Trace a little bit, except it hadn't started to show yet, maybe. I liked that idea. Really worthy.

When Trace got really sick and knew he was dying, I tried hard not to ever make Lucille mad. I'd come home some days from school, and she would be fixing supper or something special just for Trace to eat and crying. I didn't have to ask why.

Late one afternoon Laura came down the stairs crying, and Lucille hugged her and walked her out to her car with her arm around her. When I went upstairs, Trace wasn't in his hospital bed but sitting in his wheelchair, a blanket over his lap, looking out the window.

"Hello, kid." That's all he said, like he was so much older than I was because of being sick and suffering so much. He just kept sitting there looking out the window at the big, bare maple in our backyard, the leaves all gone. In bed at night awake and knowing Trace was still awake, I wanted to ask him what it felt like to die. What did you think about? Were you afraid of being embalmed and then buried?

Did you want to be conscious so that you knew you were
dying, could feel yourself die, and could look up at your family
around your bed? Or did you want to die alone, just yourself,
because nobody could stop you from dying anyway, or did
you want to be drugged so you didn't even know when you
died, and so you weren't scared? And did you expect to see a
light coming toward you or hear a familiar voice calling your
name? Or did you think your spirit would leave your body and
float up above your bed, and you could see people below you,
and yourself dead lying in the bed with your eyes closed? And
your spirit was going somewhere, but you didn't know where,
at least not for sure?

But I didn't ask these questions. Even with all the morphine
drip, Trace was still in a lot of pain, and the last weeks the pain
got so bad they had to increase the morphine, so he was in and
out of consciousness most of the time, so you couldn't talk to
him anyway.

Then one night when the lights were out and I thought
Trace was asleep or drugged out, he said, "Why do I have to
die?" His voice sounded like it wasn't connected to him or
anything, just a whisper in the dark room, like he was asking
God or somebody.

That's all Trace said, just kind of whispered it. He wasn't
crying or anything, at least not that I could hear; sometimes he
cried without making any sounds, the tears slipping down his
cheeks, glistening in the moonlight from the window, Trace
not trying to wipe them away, just lying there in his white
bed. It was like he told me he didn't want to die because I
could stop him, and all he had to do was ask, as if I were a
great doctor, an apostle, or God and could perform miracles
or something. Like he was such a great person—handsome,
intelligent, talented, and all spiritual—that he shouldn't have
to die. But that was before he got really sick and was in all the
pain, and before Grandpa and Grandma Hooper came for him

twice. But maybe not to take him with them, but just to let him know they were there in heaven waiting.

I almost said, "Maybe you won't have to die, Trace. Maybe they will invent this new medicine or you'll have one more priesthood blessing, and you'll get better, and it will be a miracle because you're supposed to go on a mission to China and convert all these people." But I didn't say that. Everything sort of transcendent, I just lay there listening to him breathe until I fell asleep.

The next morning, which was Saturday, when I walked into the kitchen, Lucille was mixing pancake batter. I thought I should say, "Trace said last night that he doesn't want to die." Like I expected her to make it so he didn't have to somehow. But I didn't say anything. At least I had that much sense. Lucille always did waffles with fresh crushed strawberries and whipped-cream topping, bacon and eggs, and fresh-squeezed orange juice on Saturday mornings.

• • •

Working back in the shaft, I decided that if I didn't make it out of the avalanche, I would write a note telling everybody how hard I'd tried. I didn't want them thinking I hadn't tried. In the spring they'd see the shaft all caved in, the pop-can exhaust hose, and the opened Suburban door, but I wanted to be sure they knew how hard I'd tried. It was important to try, to give it your best shot, because you had to have faith, like Grandpa Hooper said.

"That's what a real man does, Kyle."

I worked as long as I could, but I had to stop. I was so tired. I had to get warm. I couldn't work any longer. I didn't listen to the news. What was the point? When I sniffed the air, I smelled exhaust fumes. The smell wasn't strong, but I knew the hose had a hole somewhere. As soon as I got my hands and feet warm, I turned off the engine. To find the leak, I'd have to dig up the whole hose, but I knew I didn't have the strength, even if I could find it. It was getting harder and harder to make my body do things. I was down to two gallons of gas, so I wouldn't be able to run the engine much longer anyway.

I'd eaten all two pounds of the hamburger, one small piece at a time. I put pieces in my pockets so I had them while I was working. I couldn't believe I'd eaten the whole two pounds of raw frozen hamburger already, only it wasn't really eating, just letting it thaw in my mouth and then swallowing because I didn't chew the pieces.

As I sat in the Suburban wrapped in my quilt, I wondered what Lucille would say if she knew I'd eaten all that raw hamburger. I kind of smiled.

I'd pulled my share of fast ones on Lucille, but I didn't talk back to her or give her any sass. I'd tried that once, and she'd come down on me like a ton of bricks.

"Oh, no, you don't talk to me that way, hotshot. You talk to me; you don't sass me. I didn't take it from your brothers, and I'm not taking it from you. You understand me, Kyle?"

"I guess."

"What do you mean, you guess? Do you understand or not?"

"Oh, sure."

"Good. Say what you have to say, but no sarcasm or sass."

And then Lucille hugged me and mussed up my hair. She liked to put her fingers through my hair. She didn't care if I wore it sort of long, but on Sunday I had to wear a white shirt and tie and suit to pass the sacrament and be sure my hair was combed and my fingernails were cut and clean. Lucille always ironed my white shirt, like I might forget or something, and had it hanging up on the closet door handle Saturday night like some kind of reminder. All the boys in the Aaronic Priesthood who passed, prepared, or blessed the sacrament had to wear white shirts. The bishopric all wore white shirts, and so did nearly all the men. It was like a uniform or something, like if you didn't wear a white shirt you were some kind of special sinner because white meant purity, or righteousness, or something. I had a blue dress shirt and a red tie I wanted to wear, but Lucille put the skids under that.

"You're wearing a white shirt just like Bishop Goodmer asked you to. It's expected of boys bearing the Aaronic Priesthood and administering the sacrament. It means that at least you know it's Sunday, which is the day we go to church in this family, which may have slipped your mind. Your father and your brothers all wear white shirts on Sunday, and so are you. No argument."

"Okay, okay. You don't have to make a federal case out of it." That was something Grandpa Hooper always said.

"I'm pleased you understand."

"Oh, I do."

• • •

Leaning forward in the seat, I kept looking at my shadowy, thin, bony face in the rearview mirror, my eyes dark circles and sinking back into my head. All I wanted to do was sit curled up in my quilt, turn on the heater full blast, and not have to move ever again and not ever be cold again in my whole life.

I was so hungry. I had the can of water on the seat and kept drinking it. But it just made me feel heavy and bloated, like I was going to puke or something. I wanted to eat my candle, just sit there chewing and chewing on the wax and then swallowing it, but I knew that would be dumb. I needed the candle for light.

Shivering, I closed my eyes and imagined eating all kinds of delicious food. I'd never really been hungry before in my whole life. The mountain climber who fell and broke his leg and had to crawl down the mountain didn't have anything to eat for three days except one thin chocolate bar. I didn't know how long it took you to starve to death. In Africa and India and other places people just died on the streets, curled in the fetal position, their ribs, elbows, and skulls pushing tight against their skin. In the pictures the people walking by didn't even look down. Lucille was always telling me how grateful I should be because I had three meals a day. I tried being grateful, even telling myself, "You're grateful. You're grateful." But it didn't seem to work.

Every year Lucille sent me to Dr. Wellmen to get my annual physical, which I didn't like in the first place because I had to stand there just in my shorts, and he'd have to check me for a hernia. So ignominious. But then Dr. Wellmen was a doctor, so it was okay, I guess. I had to have a blood test. At Jefferson High you heard about kids getting an STD. Walking down the hall looking at all the girls, sometimes I thought about what would happen if I'd just kissed a girl—and that was all—who had an STD or something worse, and she had a sore on her lips and so did I, and I caught it that way. Or probably I just held hands with her, which would be perfectly natural, and we both had sores on our hands, and that's how it happened. And Dr. Wellmen would tell me to sit down after I got my clothes back on and say, "Kyle, you're in trouble, I'm afraid, son. You've got an STD."

"You mean a sexually transmitted disease?"

"Yes. Gonorrhea to be exact."

"No, I don't, I couldn't have. No, I don't. I don't have any sores." And my whole throat would go dry, my heart pounding hard like my chest was a drum.

"I'm afraid you do. There aren't always sores, at least not in the early stages. I need to know the names of all the girls you've had sex with, unless of course it was just one, which isn't very likely, typically. I have to report all this to the County

Board of Health so they can find them and treat them before this thing spreads any further. And you'll have to tell your parents of course. You're lucky it isn't AIDS or syphilis. We get that too with you kids at the high school. More than you'd think."

"But I never had sex with any girls, not even one girl, not even one. I'm not that kind of guy."

"Well, maybe you don't think you did. Maybe you were drunk at some party or high on drugs. It happens all the time."

"But I've only been drunk once in my whole life, and that was when I was fourteen, which was just for one afternoon. I've never been high. I don't do drugs, Dr. Wellmen, really. I've never been high in my whole life." And I'd stand up and give the Boy Scout sign so he'd believe me.

"Well, I'm sure you'll figure it out eventually, Kyle. I'm sorry, son, but you've got gonorrhea. I had the lab technician run the blood sample twice. It is hard to believe, a fine young man like you from a Mormon family."

And I'd try to explain how I must have gotten it by kissing a girl or maybe holding hands, but Dr. Wellmen wouldn't believe me. And I'd ask Dr. Wellmen if he couldn't give me a shot or something to cure the STD, so that nobody else had to know, especially not Frank and Lucille. And Dr. Wellmen would say of course, he'd start treatment right then, which would be so awesome, but then he'd say he still had to report all STD cases.

I tried to imagine what Lucille, Frank, Brooke, and Jed would say, and Nate and Clay, who always said they'd kick my butt up between my shoulders if I did anything really stupid, and Mark and Bishop Goodmer. Everybody in the ward and at school would know. Even probably Grandpa and Grandma Hooper and Trace, who were dead, because dead people in heaven still know about their families on Earth. It was too awful to even think about, so egregious. Having an STD changed the whole way you thought about yourself.

I'd just tell Frank and Lucille I had something important to tell them, and they'd sit down at the kitchen table probably, and Lucille would say, "Well, what have you been up to this time, Kyle? Surprise us." Which is what she always said.

"Well, I went to Dr. Wellman to get my physical today."

"Yes, we know all about that. You're not sick, are you?"

"No. But maybe a little."

"A little? What's that supposed to mean?"

"Well . . ."

"Well, what, Kyle?"

And then I'd say something like, "Well, Dr. Wellmen says I have an STD." I wouldn't say *gonorrhea* because it sounded worse than just STD or *sexually transmitted disease* either because *sexually* and *disease* were both bad. And I'd tell them I hadn't been *promiscuous*, which is a word that doesn't sound too bad. And I'd explain about holding hands with this girl and kissing her and sores and everything. And then I'd say, "It's a lot better than having AIDS, isn't it?" Which ought to make Frank and Lucille feel better.

When I'd told Mark what Grandpa Hooper had said about soldiers whoring in Korea, I said I was going to ask Tolson if *whoring* was a gerund or not. Mark just shook his head.

"Sure, ask the Vestal Virgin right during class and see what happens. She'll probably send you down to see Jagger again for being obscene in class and insulting all the girls or something. Hooper, you are so lame. How do you come up with all this stuff?"

"Oh, I don't know. I just like to think about things."

"Well, stop thinking. It's dangerous."

• • •

Leaning forward, I opened the glove compartment and took everything out. I thought there might be an old stick of gum or even a cough drop or one of Grandpa's suckers in the back.

Unwrapping the quilt, I got down on the floor and reached back under the seat. Maybe a stale cookie or half a candy bar? I got the flashlight and looked. I pulled out some old gas receipts, a sock, two McDonald's bags, but nothing to eat. I felt under the passenger seat. I pulled out more trash, and then I felt something round. I pulled it out. The sucker I'd been working on when the avalanche hit. I didn't say anything. I thought I was going to cry. It was so worthy, so magnanimous.

I washed the sucker off with some snow, wrapped up in my quilt, and sat letting the sugary cherry-flavored juice slip down my throat. I closed my eyes. It was so great. Grandpa was always taking the sucker out of his mouth to point at things or kind of wave it in the air to emphasize a point when he was telling one of his stories. Lucille said suckers were bad for my teeth.

"Thank you, Grandpa."

I turned off the light and sat in the darkness. All I wanted was to feel the sucker juice going down my throat into my stomach. Grandpa Hooper said the air force pilot in prison in Vietnam was starved for six years. He got just a bowl of watery rice or some kind of fish-head soup with fish eyes in it twice a day. I tried to imagine chewing on an eye. I didn't know how a man could be so brave.

"Where are you, Grandpa and Grandma? What are you doing? What about you, Trace?"

I smiled. I decided they must be on another planet, one just like Earth, only somehow better. People would be happier and get to do the things they'd always wanted to do and couldn't back on Earth, like go to great ski resorts, sail all over the oceans from island to island, fly their own airplane everywhere they wanted to go. If you died young, or got killed, you could get married to some terrific girl who'd died too, make love all the time, have a beautiful house, lots of money, and two or three great cars, and some kids so you had your own family. You were related to everybody somehow. And nobody ever got sick and died like Trace or got old like Grandpa Hooper. You probably had to work too, but it was work you really enjoyed.

And I wondered how long eternity was because it seemed a long time, it went on forever and never ended, and what could you do for that long? But I decided I wouldn't worry about that. It would be so gratifying to be related to old Caesar and Attila the Hun and Genghis Khan, and guys like that we'd studied about in world history, and be able to talk to them about things, because everybody was related finally. And old Gadianton, Korihor, and, of course, Laman and Lemuel in the Book of Mormon, to see how things turned out for them, if they made it at least to the telestial kingdom, or maybe got cast into outer darkness. And talk to Captain Moroni too and Nephi, and ask them why they were so righteous when they were just kids, without ever really having to try, like it was just natural or something, and wasn't it a little boring maybe sometimes?

When I was fourteen I asked Lucille if heaven was this planet or galaxy or something, but I didn't say anything about doing all the things you wanted to do on Earth after you got there. I was smarter than that.

"Oh, it will be more wonderful than you can possibly imagine."

"Great." I decided that the skiing would really have to be fantastic, nothing but three feet of new powder every day.

• • •

I chewed and sucked on the end of the sucker stick, trying to get out all the flavor.

I'd been in the avalanche a week. Had my friends already

started to forget about me? They'd be thinking about Christmas and all the fun they were going to have. I'd forgotten about kids from school who'd died or gotten killed. I'd even begun to forget about Trace a little after two years. But I knew Mark wouldn't forget me. Not Mark. I didn't think Summer would either, not for a while anyway. Summer liked to stop and talk to me in the hall all the time. It was so commodious to stand close to her and just look at her eyes, her lips, her shining hair, breathe in her perfume, or whatever it was. She'd probably stop Mark and talk to him. She'd probably ask when my folks were going to clean out my locker and tell Mark he must miss me a lot because I was such a great friend. And he'd say yes, and he'd tell her how much I liked her. And she'd say, "I liked him too. He was really nice." Or something like that. And Mark would say, "I really miss Kyle. He was such a great guy." And Summer would say, "I know."

I chewed on the sucker stick.

Lucille had given Mark a Book of Mormon to read, and he was coming to sacrament meeting, wearing a white shirt and tie of course, sitting with Lucille because I had to pass the sacrament. She introduced him to all the cute girls in the ward and had me invite him on the priests' and teachers' high adventure that summer. Bishop Goodmer was always giving Mark the glad-hand in the foyer. Lucille said Mark would make a fine missionary.

"Missionary?" I said. "The poor dope isn't even a member yet, and you've already got him on a mission."

"We'll see. The Lord moves in a mysterious way his wonders to perform."

"He sure does."

"You should be more encouraging."

"Not me. I've got my own worries."

I told Mark he'd better be careful reading the Book of Mormon because you could never knew what might happen.

"What do you mean, *happen*? All I'm going to do is read it."

"That's the problem. Don't say I didn't warn you. Lucille will be telling you to pray and ask if it's true. That's when things get ominous."

"Ominous? What do you mean, *ominous*?"

"Never mind. You wouldn't understand."

"Have you read it?"

"Sure. Well, sort of anyway."

"What's that supposed to mean? Have you prayed about it?"

"You have to be careful about that. I haven't quite finished it, so I have to wait."

"I thought you said you'd read it."

"I have, but in seminary. That's not quite the same thing as reading it at night when you're all alone and feeling all righteous."

"Why not?"

"I'm not sure."

"Brother."

At supper, Lucille would cut Mark a second piece of pie, put ice cream on it again, so she had more time to sit and talk to him about the gospel and answer all his questions. Warning him hadn't done any good, of course.

"The Book of Mormon's a very interesting book, Kyle," Mark said to me. "I like reading about things that are sacred."

"Yeah, I know. I have to get up every morning at six o'clock to go study it in seminary. Not having to get up at the crack of dawn would be interesting too."

"It's good for you. It builds character. I've liked it the times I went."

"If Bishop Goodmer hears you've been going, he'll have you in for your pre-mission interview before you're even baptized."

"Sounds interesting."

"Oh, very."

I knew all about missions. Nate went to Chile and Clay to Russia; Trace was taking Chinese so he could go to Taiwan, Hong Kong, or maybe China if it opened up. Nate and Clay both told stories about converts joining the Church and changing their whole lives, giving up drinking and smoking, paying tithing, bearing their testimonies that they knew the Church was true, their eyes full of tears. Converts brought their relatives and friends into the Church, became branch and Relief Society presidents after three months. Of course, Nate had dysentery for about six weeks, lived up in a village in the Andes at about twenty thousand feet so you almost had to be on oxygen, got eaten alive by bed bugs and head lice, developed rashes and boils. Had a cold shower, a hole in the floor for a toilet, and ate beans for breakfast, lunch, and supper. Clay slept in his overcoat and hat because there was no heat at night in their one-room St. Petersburg apartment, with rats running around. He had to break the ice in the washbasin every morning, got a bath about once a month, and was privileged to eat cabbage soup three times a day. All very inspiring. With my luck I'd end up in outer Mongolia, and I'd only be eighteen, not nineteen like Nate and Clay when they went.

I knew Lucille was just waiting for the Sunday before I turned sixteen and Bishop Goodmer had me in for the big interview to see if I was worthy to be ordained a priest and bless the sacrament because I'd be eighteen in two years and going on a mission, which was hard to believe, sort of impossible. It was no more mister nice guy. This was serious stuff, the big righteousness interview. You're sitting there across from him at his desk, your throat all dry, rubbing your sweaty hands on your pants. The older priests told us teachers that Bishop Goodmer would start out asking you about all this general stuff about school, your family, your friends, kind of buttering you up, but then he got really specific about if you'd sinned. Because some boys he interviewed to become priests repented the night before of all the sins they'd ever committed, or maybe that morning sitting in the hallway waiting for the interview. And that meant that Jesus forgave them and didn't remember their sins anymore, and if he didn't they didn't either, so they could tell Bishop Goodmer they were clean. Really nefarious.

Bishop Goodmer always started out with the Word of Wisdom, of course.

I knew he was going to say, "Kyle, when did you last smoke pot?"

"I never smoked pot, Bishop Goodmer."

"How about using crack?"

"No. Never."

"Good. When did you last get drunk?"

"When I was fourteen, but that was the only time."

"I see." Then moving on, he'd ask, "When did you last have sex?"

"Bishop, I've never had sex, honest. I'm not old enough. Gee. I won't even be sixteen until next week."

"That's wonderful, Kyle."

And he said that masturbation was a serious concern if a boy had a terrible feeling of guilt and felt totally unworthy so he even became suicidal sometimes because he couldn't be perfect like he expected or it became compulsive. A boy needed to talk to his parents, his bishop, family doctor, or some adult who could help him understand about himself better and that it was a phase most boys passed through. And did you want to talk about that? And you shook your head because Lucille had already briefed you on that particular form of amusement, which is what she called it. I didn't like the sound of the word; I thought there needed to be a nicer word.

"Good, Kyle. Good."

Bishop Goodmer asked you if you'd ever stolen anything, cheated in school, lied to your parents, taken the Lord's name in vain, or broken the law.

And then he would counsel with you and tell you to repent, and that nobody expected perfection in this life, which is what the Atonement was for, and explain all about loving everybody, including God and especially yourself. He would tell you to keep repenting, coming to all your meetings, working on keeping the commandments, seeking the Holy Ghost, building your testimony, earning your Eagle, and becoming worthy to receive the Melchizedek Priesthood when you were eighteen, be ordained an elder, go to the temple, and serve a mission, to seek true spirituality. Because you were growing up and would soon be a man. And if you ever had a serious problem to talk things over with your parents if you could. But if not, to come and talk to him or some other adult you trusted. You knelt down together by his desk and he prayed for you and for the Holy Ghost to guide you, and then shook your hand, and patted you on the shoulder. And gave you your choice of candy bars from his box and told you not to get discouraged but to keep trying because that's all the Lord expected.

"You're a fine young man, Kyle. We're all proud of you. It's a pleasure to be your bishop."

And when I got home from the interview, Lucille would ask me if I'd passed so Frank, Clay, Nate, Jed, and the bishop could ordain me a priest the next Sunday, and I'd say yes, and she'd say, "Will wonders never cease." Or something like that, which she always said. And she'd have a big chocolate cake all iced and tell me to phone Mark and tell him to come over to celebrate. Lucille was always inviting Mark to sit down and have piece of cake, pie, or milk and cookies, and talking to him about the gospel. She even invited him to the Hooper family reunion that was held in Provo every summer with a mob of relatives. But the food was great, everything potluck, whole tables loaded with fried chicken; potato, Jell-O, and fruit salads; homemade rolls; drinks; and all the desserts you could think of, all of it homemade.

"I know what I'm doing, Hooper. Your mother is really very nice."

"Yeah, well, don't say I didn't warn you."

"Tell me all about it."

Eighth Day, Saturday

The next morning I could run the engine only for about five minutes before the fumes got too strong. I didn't even have time to get my hands and feet warm. I just wanted to sit there wrapped in the quilt, not move ever again, pull the quilt up over my head, curl up. But I knew I couldn't be a quitter. I prayed.

I knew that the flashlight was getting dim, my last batteries, but leaving the Suburban ceiling light on helped some, and I still had my candle. I chewed what was left of the sucker stick, drank half a bean-can of cold water. I only had about a gallon of gas left in the tank. I climbed back up the shaft.

Grandpa Hooper had told me how miners used to take a canary in a cage down into the mines, and if it keeled over dead they got out of the mine because there was poison gas. A canary was more sensitive to gas than a human. What I needed was a canary, but even if I had one and it died in the shaft from lack of oxygen, I wouldn't be able to go anywhere. I'd just have to climb down carrying the dead canary in its cage. Of course, I could pluck it and roast it over the candle, which would be about one mouthful, very succulent. I wondered if anybody had ever eaten a roasted canary.

I worked as hard as I could in the shaft, but then the flashlight got dimmer just before I started down the shaft to go rest. I'd kept thinking I was going to break through. I'd give one last jab with the trenching tool and suddenly I wouldn't feel icy snow, just my hand and arm going up and out, smell fresh air. I'd push my head through into the sunlight. Some skier would see me climbing out and come tearing down and slam to a stop right in front of me. And he'd say he thought I was a bear and how awful I looked. I'd tell him my name, but he wouldn't believe it. I'd tell him I'd dug myself out. He'd see the hole where the shaft ended; he'd start yelling it was the Hooper kid. And the ski patrol would come and lift me on a stretcher because I'd be so weak, and there'd be this big crowd. It would be so worthy.

But I hadn't broken through. I'd kept running into heavy fir branches I had to saw through and big rocks I had to dig out. Standing there at the bottom of the shaft holding the dead flashlight, I was glad I hadn't eaten the candle; it was all I had left for light in the shaft. But I had to have more light than that. I could make a lamp out of the bean can maybe, use a wire handle to carry it up the shaft, but the candle would last only maybe an hour. I had to think about more light, really think about that, but not right then. I was so tired.

• • •

My whole body sagged; I could hardly lift my arms anymore to dig. I was dizzy, freezing. I'd never really thought about starving to death. The shaft caving in on me maybe, getting killed by the carbon monoxide, falling down the shaft and breaking my neck maybe, or cutting my head with the trenching tool and bleeding to death were possibilities. But not starving to death. It took too long. That was really funny. I smiled. It made me think about Trace. That night I'd thought Trace was asleep, and he'd said in his whispery voice, "You're a good kid, do you know that?" I didn't say anything. "You can have my Martin guitar." I still didn't know what to say. And then I knew that Trace was crying again, all quiet, but still crying. Raising myself up on my elbows, I looked over at him. Lying there in his hospital bed staring up at the ceiling, he just kept crying, but still quiet. I didn't know what to do. What are you supposed to do when your big brother, who's dying and everybody thinks is so wonderful, cries? Finally I said, "I'm glad you're my brother, Trace." I had to say something. You couldn't just lie there.

"It's okay, kid, it's okay. I don't really mind. Not anymore. Not really. It's been such a long time. It really hurts."

Lying there listening to Trace cry, sniffing, my eyes got watery. I had to keep blinking; it was really sad. Grandpa Hooper said it was all right for a man to cry. He'd seen brave men in Korea cry, some who'd even won medals, so I guess it was all right if you really had to. I still didn't think Trace was going to die. I wondered if a person died how he became just a spirit, how the spirit got out of his body, and then out of the house, maybe right through the ceiling or a wall, but maybe through an open window or door, and where it went then. Probably to another planet? Did it travel at the speed of light?

Frank and Lucille went to the funeral home to pick out Trace's casket. None of us kids went. I didn't want to go. Willie Bodlie had taken Mark and me into the casket room that time Mark and I were there. They had all these open caskets lined up, pale lights on them, soft music playing, oak caskets and cherry, and different kinds of colored metal caskets, even pink, and caskets for little kids and babies. They were all silk-lined and had pillows, although I didn't know what you'd want a pillow for if you were dead. And then of course Willie had taken us into the embalming room with the long stainless-steel table with drains, and machines that looked like pumps, and other stuff. Mark and I stayed just inside the door; we didn't want to go all the way in. It was pretty horrific seeing where they actually embalmed you.

"What are you scared of? My dad lets me go in all the time. It's interesting. I'm going to be funeral director too someday. They make a lot of money."

"Great. They deserve it. We got to go." And Mark and I got on our bikes and took off fast.

I didn't think they'd have to embalm me if I starved to death, and froze, and then thawed out, but maybe they would. "Local high-school skier starved to death while trying to dig himself out of avalanche." That's what they'd say on TV in the spring when the snow melted. They'd show shots of the ski patrol loading me on a sled, probably already in a body bag. And they'd have to do an autopsy because nobody had been there to watch me die. Just thinking about that made me want to swear, say lots worse words than *hell* and *damn*, which I'd heard Grandpa Hooper say, but I didn't.

I didn't know how long it took to starve to death, but the way I felt, I knew it couldn't take very long. The idea didn't scare me, just made me sad. It didn't seem like a very nice way to die. I'd begun to sense things slowing down for me. I felt older, like I wasn't a kid anymore.

Maybe that's what happens when you start to die. Trace seemed older the last few weeks before he died, like he knew a lot of things he hadn't known before. I thought again about those things I'd do if I didn't die and if I got out—earn my Eagle, get a 4.0, practice the piano, never swear again, not think about girls so much, or be such a smart ass all the time, go on a mission to India or somewhere else really tough, and be the assistant to the mission president like Nate. I really would.

• • •

I climbed back into the Suburban and wrapped myself in my quilt. I had the ceiling light on, but I didn't turn on the engine because of the fumes. I probably had less than a gallon of gas left anyway. The Suburban really sucked it up.

"At least I'm not dead." I listened to myself say that. "I'm not dead yet. I'm not." I didn't say it loud but whispered it, like I was trying to convince myself.

Thinking about being dead, which I was glad I wasn't, I thought about how many times I'd gone to the temple to be baptized for the family dead. Standing in the font, I'd see this relative's name, who'd be about five hundred years old if he was alive, come up on the screen, and Nate or Clay would say the baptismal prayer with the name and then baptize me for him. And Lucille would be sitting outside the glass window, smiling. And then afterward you had to be confirmed for each one so they could become members of the Church and go on progressing forever, which I guess they wanted to do.

And your relative, the great-great-great-great-great uncle, or whoever it was, was supposed to have been waiting for hundreds of years, or maybe a thousand. Your dead relatives wanted to be baptized so they could get out of spirit prison and start progressing, and they were watching you and were so grateful. At least that's what Glimmer told us in seminary. And heaven was supposed to be full of hundreds of millions of people, maybe even billions, wanting to be baptized. And if they were members of your family, they kept coming to you in dreams and visions and other ways trying to get you to research their names and do their temple work.

Mark was in seminary that morning. Walking out afterward, he said, "I dream about my dad, but he's never come to actually see me. Man, that would be so great. Do you think that could really happen, Kyle?"

"Sure, I guess. Why not? That's what they're supposed to do sometimes. Just ask old Lucille, she knows all about that kind of stuff."

"It would be so great."

Lucille was always working on our family history and taking family names to the temple. And if you did, when you died all your relatives would be waiting for you on the other side of the veil or somewhere to thank you, whole crowds of them, and wanting all the family news. But if you didn't do their temple work, didn't get the lead out, they wouldn't be waiting, or appear to you when you were dying, or at least I guess they wouldn't. They'd probably wait at the veil and say something, but I couldn't decide what. They couldn't be mean or mad at you, could they, in heaven? Maybe they'd just be grateful you were dead too, finally, and say they were glad you finally made it, or something like that.

"Now wasn't that a wonderful spiritual experience, Kyle? Think of all those grateful family members." Lucille always said something like that when we came out of the temple.

"Oh, just really wonderful, Mom."

Remembering being baptized for the dead with Trace made me think about him. Lucille didn't clean out Trace's closet space and drawers right after his funeral. I guess it made our room less lonely for her. It was okay with me. She asked me if I wanted to move into another bedroom, but I said no. She said she'd clean out Trace's stuff someday, but she couldn't do it then, and she still hadn't. I figured she wouldn't take all my stuff out either if I didn't make it. I guess it would still be Trace's and my room, sort of.

I was glad Lucille hadn't told me I had to grow into Trace's clothes. I really didn't want any of them, even his sharp ties, shirts, and blazers. It would feel funny to wear a dead person's clothes. I didn't want Laura, Trace's girlfriend, to say when she saw me at school or at the mall or somewhere, maybe a dance, "That was one of Trace's favorite jackets. He really looked nice in it." Or maybe seeing me way down the hall in the shadows, she'd think I was Trace resurrected or something and come back for a short, pleasurable visit just with her.

Standing looking at myself in my full-length mirror at night with all the lights out, kind of mysterious, just in my shorts and T-shirt, checking out my abs, I thought I might see Trace standing behind me, smiling. Or I'd hear him say my name across the half-dark room, Trace come back to tell me what being dead was like because we were brothers, and he thought I'd be curious, because he ought to know, and maybe warn me about a few things. I didn't know why he wouldn't; in seminary and Sunday school they talked about the dead coming back in dreams and things to leave messages and warn people. But that didn't happen.

Lying in bed I wondered what Trace was doing in heaven, if he was dating girls, living with Grandpa and Grandma Hooper, going to school. Or was he all dressed in white in some big choir or something standing there all day singing praises, probably singing solos, being all spiritual, which, if he was, sounded pretty dreary and nothing to get excited about. Or maybe because he was so righteous they made him a missionary and sent him to preach repentance to the spirits in spirit prison, which also sounded pretty dreary. But with my luck I'd probably be one he'd be preaching to. And he'd see me and say, "Well, Kyle, I'm not surprised." And I'd say, "Me either." And after I got out of prison I'd probably end up in the telestial kingdom anyway finally, but I figured I'd have lots of company. I'd even heard of returned missionaries who, like Grandpa Hooper said, went off the rails—drinking, smoking, whoring, doing drugs, viewing pornography. So invidious and not something you'd think an elder would ever do after serving as a missionary for two years.

Of course, Nate, Clay, and other returned missionaries explained all about missions to me, especially tracting. The very first morning your trainer, whose name is Moroni or Nephi or something, which isn't exactly encouraging, is up at five because he's so righteous, so you have to get up too.

But there's no place to take a shower, which you get once a week if you're lucky. So you just wash your face and shave in cold water, and eat a bowl of something you don't even know the name of, but it isn't too bad. You study this foreign language you studied for weeks in the MTC and can't even pronounce, old Moroni correcting your pronunciation on every word, making you say it over and over again for a solid hour, probably two. Then you have this long kneeling prayer asking the Lord to lead you to the honest in heart so they'll accept the gospel. You tell Moroni you'll just watch him for the first day tracting, or better, maybe the whole week. He just smiles. He takes the first door and then tells you that you get the next one. You say no because you can't even speak the language, but he just rings the doorbell. When the lady comes to the door, Moroni just stands there like he's struck dumb, and you don't know what to say.

You think you're going to wet your pants. And the lady says yes, may I help you, in German, Hungarian, Chinese, Japanese, or whatever language it is. You understand about two words, and you have this door approach you've memorized, and you try that, Moroni not helping you of course. The lady asks if you're Americans, which is a word you understand, so you say yes in English, and then in Hungarian. And then the lady says in perfect English that Americans are nice people, thanks you, and closes the door, and you stand there feeling like an idiot.

The next two doors get slammed in your face, the one guy hollering at you all the way down the stairwell, although you don't know what he's saying, just that he doesn't like you very much. And you know you can't do this eight hours a day for two years, you just can't. And then Moroni tells you that you have a meeting with investigators to present a lesson, and after that lunch with a widowed sister who's a great cook, and in the afternoon you're going to go back to the apartment, change to work clothes, and spend the next three days helping paint this orphanage run by Catholic nuns. So you think you'll probably live and Moroni might be human after all. But right now you need to find a bathroom quick, and you ask old Moroni about that possibility.

That evening back in the apartment, you've decided that you might even like Elder Moroni and so you tell him about your girlfriend Evangeline who's waiting for you, a real lovely, and show Moroni her picture. He smiles, hands it back, and says very nice. You went with Evangeline your whole senior year, took her to all the dances, parties, games, and everything, bought her all these expensive birthday and Christmas gifts, and you know you want to marry her because she's got this perfect body and everything. She wants you to go on your mission because she loves you so much and wants all your sons to be missionaries. On Sunday nights you sit in front of the fire and read scriptures to each other. But she won't even hold hands after you get your mission call; she's very brave, smiling through her tears.

According to all the missionary stories you've heard, Evangeline promises to write you at least twice a week and send you goodies, which she does the first month you're in the MTC, but then she only writes once the next week, and none your last week in the MTC. Which you understand because she's busy as a freshman at BYU majoring in marriage and family life. You agreed before you left that Evangeline should date maybe once a month so she wouldn't be so sad missing you, and she writes and tells you about this recently returned missionary named Oswald who's very nice and cheers her up, which you think is okay. So every day you're waiting for a letter, and then you come back to the apartment, and there it is under the door where your landlady put it. Hands trembling, sitting down on your bunk, you open it carefully.

It starts out Dear Elder, so you know something is up. And Evangeline says how much she admires and respects you, but

she and old Oswald are engaged to be married, and she knows
it's what the Lord wants her to do because Oswald is such a
spiritual giant and they're so much in love and he's going to
be a dentist or maybe a chiropractor. Evangeline knows you'll
understand, and she's sure you'll find some wonderful sister
returned missionary who will love you as much as she loves
Oswald.

You sit there on your bunk staring at the letter, and Moroni
asks you what's wrong because you look a little pale and have
tears in your eyes. You tell him, and he smiles and gets the
letter his ex-girlfriend sent him, which you read, and he tells
you she already has a baby and another one on the way. Moroni
pats you on the shoulder and tells you you'll live. He says
he'll treat you to supper at this great little restaurant he knows,
which should help with the terrible pain you're suffering, and,
still sitting there on your bunk holding Evangeline's letter, you
smile sort of and say thanks.

• • •

Eyes closed, trying to figure out how I could get more light
in the shaft, thinking as hard as I could, I listened to Crystal
Creek; very faint but I could hear it if I really listened. Grandpa
Hooper really was a great cheese fisherman. As a kid I carried
the package of cream cheese. You molded a little ball to put on
your hook. Mark came with us sometimes.

The Eskimos ate raw fish, so did Japanese people. Frank
ate raw pickled herring sometimes. So it couldn't be that
bad if you just took little bites and swallowed it fast, like the
frozen hamburger, not really appetizing, but okay under the
circumstances, very nourishing. All I needed was some cheese
and my fishing pole. I kept thinking about how I could rig a
pole and get some bait. Really thinking; this was important.

I sat up.

I had string and I could make a hook out of wire. But I needed bait. I thought about that; I sure didn't have any cream cheese. I sat there thinking and looking around, saw my grocery box. Orange peel looked like cheese, but I'd eaten all the orange peels. Maybe I might have missed some. "Please, please, I'm so hungry."

I got down on the floor with the candle and found one piece I'd missed. So propitious. "Thank you." I made the hook, sharpened the point with my file. I tied a small bolt on the string for a sinker. I cut the orange peeling into three small pieces and put one piece on the hook. I missed the first bite, baited again, and caught about a one-pound rainbow on the second. So gladsome, so spectacular. I cleaned the trout and, using a razor blade because my Scout knife was dull, I cut each side into three strips and warmed them a little bit over the candle. I just couldn't eat them cold.

I wished I had some of the catsup left to kill the taste, but I was so hungry I didn't really care. Holding a strip of warm trout in my hands like a cob of corn, I bit the meat away from the skin and big bones. I knew I couldn't eat the skin. I thought I was going to puke as I worked to swallow the greasy, rubbery pieces of trout. I just bit off small pieces, didn't chew, swallowed them fast like the hamburger, kept drinking water, forcing myself not to puke. Not very toothsome, but it didn't taste too bad if I drank a lot of water.

Spitting out the hair bones, I ate the whole trout except for the skin, head, tail, and guts. Grandpa Hooper told me that the American colonel in the bamboo cage in Vietnam even ate the fish heads in his soup he was so hungry, so I didn't have it so bad, at least not yet.

"I guess it just depends on how hungry you are, Kyle baby."

Lucille was always telling me faith-promoting stories about the starving Mormon pioneers fighting the hordes of crickets to save their wheat crops and the seagulls coming to eat all the crickets, which was a miracle, which was why they had the seagull monument on Temple Square in Salt Lake all made out of gold. Brother Glimmer told us in seminary how the Indians used to go down to the Great Salt Lake to fill their willow baskets with crickets. Millions of crickets flying over the lake fell in, the wind blowing them ashore in windrows, so they were easy to gather in big baskets. The Indians mashed the crickets and mixed them with dried wild fruit and seeds to make cricket bars. Very nutritious, and already salted.

I was going to tell Lucille that the pioneers would have been better off if they'd gathered up all the crickets, even gone down to Great Salt Lake to get them, and made cricket bars, and forgotten about the wheat, or at least mixed the mashed crickets with the wheat they saved, but I knew how far that would get me. They should have a cricket monument on Temple Square too, but I sure didn't mention that idea to Lucille either. She'd have killed me. Lucille was a great believer in miracles.

Still hungry, I caught one more planter with my last piece of orange peel and ate it. The guts from the first trout were gone, just a stain in the snow, so I knew the mink had got them. It was okay; he was hungry too. I'd caught two trout and figured I could probably catch more. The hole was probably full of planters. I wrapped the guts from the last trout in aluminum foil and put them in the Suburban. I was out of orange peel, but I figured I could use pieces of fish guts for bait; they looked like worms.

I sat in the Suburban wrapped in the quilt. Eating the trout had helped, but I still didn't feel very strong. I shivered, my teeth chattering, but I could still stop if I wrapped my arms around my chest and pulled tight, clamped my jaws. In the class the paramedics said that one way to check if a person was dead from hypothermia was to pull his arms straight. If they curled back he was still alive. Dead people couldn't do that. I rubbed and rubbed my feet and toes, but they were still cold and turning white. Every time I woke up in the middle of the night, I turned on the light to see if the ends of my fingers had started to turn black yet.

Sitting there in the darkness, thinking about getting more light, I thought about school and what Mark and everybody were doing. It surprised me how much I missed school and all the things I used to do.

Sometimes you heard about girls getting pregnant and all teary-eyed, telling their boyfriends right in the hall or maybe right in class. I'd look around my biology class when we were studying about reproductive cycles and wonder what it would be like when you were maybe a senior to see some girl you'd had sex with the night before in your car or at a party or someplace, and think she might be pregnant or something. What would you do if she came up to you a month later in the hall at school and said, "I'm pregnant. I took the test four times. It went all blue. And you're the father. We have to get married."

And then she would put her arms around you and start to cry. "I love you so much, Kylie. I know we'll be so happy." Or her dad called your dad at the office with the happy news, or the doorbell rang on some otherwise pleasant evening after a hard day at school just when you're sitting down to a nice supper with apple pie a la mode for dessert, which was one of your favorites. And you went to the door, and there she was all teary-eyed, standing there with her dad, and probably her mom too, and her dad said, "Young man, I want to speak to your father."

Wouldn't that be gratifying, just because one of your sperm made a wrong turn and accidentally banged into one of her eggs, or whatever they are, like she was maybe a chicken or a duck? You could say you wanted a blood test because maybe she'd been sleeping with some other guys too, but you knew that she hadn't, because she loved you so much, so that wouldn't work.

What would Lucille say, Frank, my whole family? Mark? Mark's mom? Summer? The neighbors? Everybody at church, at school—Miss Tolson, who you know really kind of likes you, and all your other buddies and also the girls who think you're so cute? Because when you didn't get married in the temple, everybody in the ward would know why. You can't even bear to think about it, having to marry a girl you didn't even really love who was already pregnant, because you couldn't even think about persuading her to have an abortion because that would be murder, and even worse.

You wouldn't be a returned missionary, have a big wedding reception with lots of gifts and all your former missionary companions congratulating you and telling you what a knockout your wife was and wishing you all the happiness in the world. And your trainer standing there with his totally pregnant wife holding a one-year-old kid and smiling at you, and your mission president and his wife, probably. If you did have a reception your wife would probably have to wear black or at least gray, maybe red, because white meant pure or virginal or something. And you wouldn't be going on any honeymoon because what was the point. And they'd probably excommunicate you anyway.

And you'd have to live with her parents or maybe Frank and Lucille, sleep in your old bedroom in your old bed where you always slept alone before, because you were broke and still in high school, and probably have to get a job working nights at McDonald's or Taco Bell. And every day she'd get bigger and bigger, and maybe she'd keep going to school so she could graduate too, everybody seeing her. The whole class turning to look at you when Tolson read one of her romantic poems you used to like about how great love was. Or maybe the scene where old Juliet finds Romeo dead, and decides she has to kill herself too because she loves him so much. Yeah, sure. Mark and your friends asking when the happy day was and did you want a boy or a girl, or maybe twins, and what we were going to name it.

And you knew you didn't want to be a father and wondered what you'd do when you had to hold it and tell people it was yours when they asked whose baby it was because you were obviously too young to be a father. You'd have to change it, feed it a bottle, and get up in the middle of the night because it had been crying for six hours straight with colic, or whatever that stuff is called. I didn't want anybody to think of me as the kind of kid who slept around and got girls pregnant, especially not my family, including Grandpa and Grandma Hooper and Trace, even if they were dead, because they'd know, and Mark, and everybody. Like I'd betrayed them all, wasn't the kid they thought I was, although I knew they'd still love me of course. But I was going to have to watch it.

• • •

Swallowing against the fish taste, eyes open, trying to see in the darkness, I kept trying to figure out how I was going to get more light. The only power I had was the battery. I had to use the battery in some way. If I didn't break through the surface before I used up the two inches of candle I had left, it would be good night nurse, which is what Grandpa Hooper always said. I couldn't dig in the dark.

It didn't bother me so much anymore that I might not make it. I'd kind of gotten used to the idea of dying. Trace did, while he was still conscious those last weeks. The morphine drip killing most of the pain I guess, he just lay in his hospital bed looking out the window and waiting, not sitting up in his wheelchair anymore. The mountain climber who fell and broke his leg said he wasn't afraid of dying; he just didn't want to die alone. He cried a lot. I could understand that. If I started bawling, I probably wouldn't be able to stop.

One night in our bedroom, the lights out, I thought I heard Trace call my name. I raised up in bed. Then I heard him again, "Kyle," his voice a whisper.

"What? Trace?"

"Be with me."

"What?"

"Be with me. Please."

I got out of bed and went over and got under the covers.

"Hold me, Kyle. Please."

I put my arms around Trace, his head on my shoulder.

Not crying, he whispered, "Hold me tight, Kyle, please. Don't let me go. Don't let me go."

I held Trace a long time, felt his ribs though his thin flesh, until he fell asleep. I didn't ever tell Lucille or anybody. I didn't think I should. Trace died two weeks later.

• • •

I was dizzy most of the time now. Everything had started to get kind of vague. I had to keep slapping my arms and hands against my body. I knew I couldn't turn on the engine anymore, even if I had gas.

I wondered what freezing to death was like. You just gradually can't feel your body anymore, the cold going deeper and deeper into your heart and lungs and everything freezes. Even your brain, and your tongue and your eyes crystallizing. And that's just the way it is. You don't know it's happening, so you aren't even scared.

I had very little feeling in the ends of my toes and fingers now that I couldn't get them really warm. I was shivering all the time. I knew it was the beginning of frostbite and hypothermia. I kept wrapping my arms around my chest and pulling as tight and hard as I could to try to stop the shivering.

How was I going to get more light in the shaft? I had to

have it or I was toast. I had to think about my resources. I had the ceiling bulb and the fixture. I could pull those to use in the shaft. I could cut the wire to connect for power, but I'd need at least forty feet of wire to connect to that hot lead. Where was I going to get that much wire? I tried to kind of imagine the whole Suburban in my mind, think about it one part at a time, the engine, battery, ceiling, inside, back, wiring, imagine everything, like Grandpa Hooper always said to do, but praying at the same time too. Wire. I needed wire. I sat there. I sat up straight.

"You're an idiot, Kyle Hooper, an idiot."

The Suburban was full of small-gauge wire for the parking and back-up lights. I'd helped Grandpa Hooper replace bulbs. I could get all the wire I needed and a bulb and fixture too. I wouldn't need the ceiling stuff.

Pushing off the quilt, I turned on the light. I looked at the clock. It didn't matter what time it was. I couldn't remember if was day or night anymore. The darkness was always there. I looked at the scratches on the dash; I made one more. My eighth day. I crawled in back and got the tools I needed from the toolbox.

I crawled down the tunnel to the back of the Suburban. I lit the candle. Working slowly, fumbling, no feeling in my fingers, I took out the screws and pulled off the parking and directional light covers. I took out one light socket with the wire still attached. I twisted the bulb out and put it in my zippered chest pocket to keep it safe. I pulled the wires until a connection broke somewhere. I needed more wire. I took off the other parking and directional light covers and pulled those wires.

Dragging the wire, I crawled back to the front of the Suburban. Fumbling, dropping things, I connected all my pulled wires using electrician's tape and tied them tight with string. I figured I had about thirty feet. I pulled the fabric around the ceiling light, cut the wire leading down to the rear light, the front light still burning, and spliced it to my wire.

I took the bulb out of my pocket. I started screwing it into the socket. I knew I had to have faith. I closed my eyes. I twisted the bulb the rest of the way in. Opened my eyes, saw the lit bulb.

"Thank you. Thank you, God. Thank you, Jesus. Thank you, Grandpa Hooper." I didn't say it out loud, just whispered it, choking back the tears. I knew I was having faith.

I'd have enough light to dig with now. I should have thought about it before and not had to worry about the flashlight. Dumb.

I ran the wire out the open window, coiling it on the snow at the bottom of the shaft. I cut some forked sticks and pushed these into the sides of the shaft every five or six feet to hold the wire. I had to be careful with the splices or they'd pull apart.

After I got the wire strung, I'd spent the whole day fixing the light. I was worn out, could hardly move. I had to get some sleep.

That night I dreamed of dancing downstairs in the family room with Lucille and her lifting one hand to run her fingers through my hair.

"The girls are going to like your beautiful hair, Kyle. Silly girls." She always said that and how the whole family would miss me when I went on my mission right after I graduated from high school. And how wonderful it was that I could go at eighteen because some boys who were planning on missions kind of slipped away from the Church before they turned nineteen, which used to be the age for missionaries. And too many boys who knew they were going on missions at the end of their college freshman year didn't study hard because they were just waiting to go and wanted to wait till they got back to pick a major.

"It'll be wonderful for you, Kyle. You'll be just out of

seminary. Boys eighteen and out of high school want to leave home and be on their own. It will be a great maturing experience. When you get back you'll know what you want to major in. But most important of all you'll be preaching the gospel every day and see how it changes converts' lives, and how it changes your life, and you'll have a firm testimony because you'll know the gospel is true and be serious about life."

I didn't say anything about my long-lost youth or anything. I was smarter than that.

I'd dreamed the night before about going to have my missionary interview with President Smyles, who was about a hundred years old and had been on about six missions. He didn't ask specific questions like Bishop Goodmer about if you'd been chaste, drank, or smoked, or anything like that, or had all this stuff you needed to confess. He figured your bishop had taken care of all the minor things. He asked you to describe your testimony and why you wanted to serve the Lord for two years, and if you'd been studying a foreign language all through junior and senior high school so you'd be prepared to be the Lord's servant. He wanted to know how many times you'd read the Book of Mormon, if you'd gone to seminary all four years, and how many scriptures you had memorized and to repeat about fifty of them. The guys who'd been interviewed said if you showed up without your missionary haircut or not dressed in your missionary suit and carrying your missionary scriptures, President Smyles nailed you and sent you back home and told you to return when you were ready for your interview.

And he asked you if you were willing to get up early every morning to study the gospel, to obey your mission president and be humble and receptive to the Spirit, and if you would tract and meet with investigators ten hours a day, and keep all the mission rules for two whole years. The guys said that

President Smyles didn't sit behind his desk with you on the other side, but sat in a chair knee to knee with you, looked you straight in the eyes, and, when you answered his questions, you'd better not lie or even blink, because he'd know.

Ninth Day, Sunday

When I woke up, I turned on the dash lights, just sat there not wanting to move, shivering in the quilt. I saw the scratches on the dash. Eight. It was my ninth day in the avalanche. It all seemed like one long night. Reaching up, I took the keys out of the ignition and made another scratch. I put the keys back in the ignition. I didn't know why.

Sunday. Lucille always woke me up early so I wouldn't be late for church, and we picked up Mark. Everyone at church had been so kind when Trace died. The Relief Society sisters brought food every day, just like the neighbors. On Sunday members I didn't even know stopped me to shake hands and say how sorry they were.

Then I realized it was Christmas Eve day. I had to close my eyes tight and not think about it. In Sunday school two weeks ago we'd talked about Jesus being born and everything and his raising Lazarus from the dead. I liked the idea, but I guessed it would take a lot of faith, just to say come on out, Lazarus, and he'd just come out of the grave with all the people standing around watching. It would have been kind of embarrassing if old Lazarus hadn't climbed out, but of course he did because Jesus was Jesus. Lucille liked stories that showed a lot of faith, as if she still needed to strengthen her faith because of Trace dying and everything. Lucille would look at me across the Sunday dinner table after we'd had one of these long discussions when she was trying to explain to me how important faith was, and I wouldn't say anything because I didn't know what to say. I'd just nod my head.

"We have to have faith as a family, Kyle. We all have to have faith." I'd nod my head.

I tried to catch another trout using a piece of trout gut. I fished for an hour before I gave up. I figured I must have caught all the rainbows, and the German browns were too smart to bite. I was so hungry. I figured if the fighter pilot in Vietnam could eat fish soup, I could too. I could cook it with the candle, which I didn't need because I had light in the shaft. With snow I washed the fish guts I'd saved from the last planter I'd caught. I cut them in small pieces so they looked like meat. I smashed the head with the hammer and cut it into small pieces too, even the eyes. I was really hungry. I put it all in the bean can with just enough water to cover it. I lit the candle and cooked it until it was hot and a little bit like soup. It tasted a little beany but mostly fishy, but it wasn't too bad. I didn't chew it; I drank it fast. It was warm going down. I felt a little stronger. Not exactly succulent, but okay. Drinking my soup made me think about Lucille; she made great soups right from scratch.

If I made it out of this alive, I knew I had to watch myself and not do anything *really* stupid. Guys got girls pregnant, got drunk every weekend, were on drugs, got busted for robbing some house looking for cash. They got hooked on pornography, even watching it in class on their phones or laptops, had no idea about sacred things. Both Nate and Clay told me that if I ever did anything that stupid they'd break my neck, or something worse. My first day in class my freshman year, teachers, who'd probably been teaching at Jefferson High for a hundred years or more, would look up from the roll and ask if I was related to Trace, Nate, Clay, or Brooke Hooper. And then, giving me the evil eye, they'd say that if I was as good a student as Brooke or Trace, I wouldn't have anything to worry about. They didn't say that about Nate or Clay.

Nate was the only one home the afternoon Mark and I got just a little drunk on the six-pack we bought by pooling our resources. Nate threw me in a cold shower with my clothes on, and after I changed, he made me put my wet clothes in the dryer and then stick them in the dirty clothes so Lucille wouldn't get suspicious and start asking questions.

"So what are you going to do, become the town drunk?"

"We just had a couple of beers."

"I don't care how many you had, you start drinking and I'll kick your butt up around your ears, and that'll be just for starters."

"I guess you never drank beer, did you?"

"It doesn't matter what I did, you dimwit. And don't you let Mom find out you've been drinking either. She's got enough to worry about with Trace sick and Dad gone all the time. You start drinking and smoking pot and you'll end up in juvenile court and probably jail."

"I'm not going to tell Lucille. You think I'm nuts? I don't smoke pot either. Besides I don't think I feel so hot. I think I'm going to go lie down."

Nate's favorite term for me was "dimwit"; Clay liked "knucklehead." Trace had called me "kid," sometimes "little brother." Lucille said that none of us boys were lilies of the valley, not even Trace, which I was surprised to hear. She said at least we hadn't become drug addicts, Silver High drunks, gotten a variety of girls pregnant on a rotating basis, committed any felonies, or left the Church, and Nate and Clay had somehow managed to serve honorable missions, for which she would be eternally grateful. Nate being assistant to the president was kind of frosting on the cake, sort of, I guess.

I just knew what Lucille would say if she heard I'd gotten

drunk. She'd probably wait till I'd eaten supper and was just starting on my dessert, a big slice of chocolate cake with her inch-thick frosting.

"Well, Kyle, decided to take up drinking, have you? Be an alcoholic by the time you're sixteen, maybe? How very interesting. We'll have to get you into rehabilitation, won't we. That might help."

"Mom, I only had about three beers. Really. It's the first time."

"Well. It's a start, isn't it? And Mark, I'm surprised at him. You're a wonderful example for a Mormon boy, aren't you, leading poor Mark astray?"

"Mom, please. I won't ever do it again. I promise."

"Well, finish your chocolate cake, Kyle. You need to keep your strength up, and then we'll have a long talk about your reformed life and how you're going to spend your school nights and long Saturdays for the next few months."

"Mom, please."

"Maybe you need another slice, a small one."

• • •

I started working in the shaft again. I was dizzy all the time. I was too weak to keep climbing down and back up to fill my lungs with fresh air. I knew that part of the dizziness was because I was so weak and hungry. My gloves were wet and coming apart. I had no feeling in my feet, no matter how long I rubbed them. The ends of my fingers and toes were turning grayish with frostbite. I looked in the rearview mirror to check my nose and ears, but it smeared when I scraped off the frost.

I drank more water. I heated it over the candle to make it warm, and then ate the rest of the candle, about an inch. It was all I had left. I had to chew on it like gum and then swallow the chewed pieces.

In the shaft I ran into a whole layer of sheared-off spruce branches that slowed me down, and some big rocks. It was the first time I hit a lot of big rocks all together. I had to dig each one out and drop it down the shaft. And then I hit a big spruce, the trunk maybe thirty inches thick, with big limbs. I knew it had helped keep the Suburban from being crushed, but I knew I couldn't cut through it with the bow saw, or even the heavy limbs. I didn't have the strength, and the bow saw was too small. I stuck the trenching tool in the side of the shaft. I lay back against the wall looking up, sort of comatose I guess.

"You ain't going to make it, Kyle Frank Hooper. You're toast, old buddy." I heard myself say that. It made me sad, but I smiled, faintly. It was okay. I'd given it everything I had. At Trace's funeral one of the speakers had said that Trace was appointed unto death. I didn't know exactly what that meant, but I guessed he was. I guessed maybe I was too. But it was okay.

I felt sad for everybody. Earlier I'd felt so sad for myself, but now I felt sad for everybody else, especially Lucille because it had been so hard for her when Trace died, but she still believed in the Church, she had so much faith. And I knew she'd still have faith if I didn't make it. Mine and Trace's bedroom would be so empty. She'd taken out the hospital bed and put Trace's bed back in the day after he died. The beds would always be made, but no clothes hanging in the closets, the dresser drawers empty, Trace's Martin in the case in the corner, my weight-lifting outfit just sitting there, me and Trace all smiling and happy in our photos on the cork board. I didn't think Lucille would haul my weights off to Good Will. She'd want to think of me using them, my muscular body all shiny with sweat.

I felt sorry for Frank too. I wished he'd hugged me like Lucille did. I wished he'd earned a couple million bucks and been happy and been home more. I wished we'd done a lot of things together. It would have been awesome. I'd thought so much about how it was going to be so great to dig my way out of the avalanche and go home and surprise everybody and make them all happy and then go to school the next morning and be on TV and everything. And I was going to do all those great things I'd planned on doing and be such a good person for the rest of my life, like earning my Eagle. But now I wasn't going to do any of those things. But it was okay. You didn't always get what you wanted in this life. Like Grandpa Hooper said, you had to take the good with the bad. You didn't blame God or anybody else. You just took it like a man.

I wouldn't be on the ski patrol. Girls really went for the guys on ski patrol. They'd sit up at the lodge at night around the big fireplace, all cozy and warm, the girls taking off their jackets and boots and pulling their legs up on the couch, lying back smiling, maybe reaching up to kiss the guy on the nose or maybe the ear. And the guy would wrap his ski jacket around her, or maybe his sweater, so she'd be all snuggly and warm. So worthy. I'd come over from the cabin at night just to watch for a while, maybe pick up a few pointers, but Lucille always called me on my phone to come back and go to bed. You'd think I was twelve instead of almost sixteen.

I wouldn't be going on a mission or to State for college when I got back either. Lucille didn't push us to go to BYU but wanted us to live in the dorms for the first year and then in an apartment.

"The Y is a reasonably good undergraduate school of course, but I'd rather have you meet all kinds of people and professors, not just people who believe like you do. You need the challenge, learn to stand on your own two feet, find out what you really believe, or think you believe. State's been a good school for your brothers and sister. Other kids need the Y more than you do. At State you've got in-state tuition, an institute, and it's close enough so I can keep an eye on you. On an occasional Sunday if you're hungry and want a break from dorm food and need to wash your clothes, you can drop by. Of course, you have to get accepted at State first, don't you."

And Lucille would always look at me when she said that, because Nate and Clay were already at State, and Brooke had graduated. Of course Trace would probably have gotten a full-ride scholarship to Stanford or Harvard or someplace, if he hadn't perished. I figured I could get into State with B's; Nate and Clay got in and they weren't exactly stellar scholars at Jefferson High. I planned to really start studying in college. I wanted to go to medical school or something, have plenty of cash coming in, maybe law school. But probably not dental school; being a dentist would be pretty dreary, looking in mouths all day.

But sitting leaning against the shaft wall thinking about all these things, I knew I couldn't just give up, quit, climb back down the shaft and wrap up in my quilt and turn off the light and just sit there waiting in the darkness. I couldn't just do that.

"No excuses, Kyle. You just keep trying." That's what Grandpa Hooper always said, and then he'd tell me a story like the one about the guy who picked up a box of dynamite caps that exploded and blew off both his hands and blinded him in both eyes. And he still made it, got married, had kids, kept a job, and never complained, because he had faith. Grandpa Hooper wouldn't want me to just quit. He wouldn't want me to do that. Not just quit, not abandon my faith.

Looking up at the big trunk of the spruce tree, I knew I could dig a horizontal shaft, a kind of tunnel, until I got past the spruce and then go up again. I still had a little strength left. Maybe that's all it would take, go up another two or three feet, maybe just a foot, and I'd be out, which would be about twenty feet altogether. I could try to do that. I knew the hypothermia and frostbite were starting to take over. I might just freeze to death right there in the shaft, just slowly stop moving and freeze. That's where they'd find me, my body, and they'd know how hard I'd tried.

I had to make myself move.

I could dig the horizontal shaft kneeling. It would be easier than going straight up. I pulled the trenching tool out of the side of shaft and started. I worked very slowly.

When I got dizzy, I'd lie down on the floor of the shaft to rest and then start digging again. I put spruce boughs on the bottom of the shaft so that my stomach and chest didn't get so cold.

I cut the shaft at right angles away from the big spruce.

It was almost dark in the horizontal shaft. I'd run out of wire. I couldn't bring my light with me all the way. I still had the big spruce above me. And then I ran into a whole wall of spruce limbs. I cut to the right and to the left in the dim light, but I couldn't get around them. They were thick and frozen with snow. The old prisoner in *The Count of Monte Cristo* had dug in the wrong direction for twenty years.

I wasn't mad at God. How could I be mad at him? I knew he'd helped me, him and the Holy Ghost of course, and Grandpa Hooper. Maybe I was like Trace, and there were things God wanted me to do in heaven or someplace, although I couldn't figure out what that was because I wasn't all spiritual like Trace. Maybe he wanted me to mow lawns and clear snow off sidewalks and do other things. Grandpa and Grandma Hooper hadn't come for me like they did for Trace, but I knew they'd be waiting for me, which was okay. I knew that Trace was kind of an unusual person, and had suffered so much, been in all that pain for months, which is why they'd come for him, everything all celestial. But maybe Trace would be standing there too, because he was my brother. Maybe he would just cheer me up a little, help me figure things out. It would be so worthy.

I just lay there on my back in the shaft. It felt good just

to finally know I'd done all I could, be able to quit, just lie there and know I didn't have to dig anymore. That's what the Alaskan miner in the story did who broke through the ice and got his feet wet. He just sat down on a log and let himself finish freezing to death. He'd tried to get his dog to come close so he could kill it and put his hand in the guts to get them warm so he could strike a match and start a fire, but the dog wouldn't come close enough. I was glad the dog was that smart. I knew I could never do something like that to Sadie.

"You're okay, Kyle Frank Hooper. You're okay. You gave it all you had. You're okay. You don't have to be afraid. Trace wasn't, not really, not at the end. You get used to things."

I was sorry for Frank and Lucille and Nate, Clay, and Brooke, and all my relatives, and all my friends, especially Mark and Summer. I was sorry I couldn't just walk into the vestal virgin's—Miss Tolson's—room. She'd be standing at the chalkboard writing something on it, and then she'd turn around and there I'd be.

"Why, Kyle, you're alive. How nice. How very nice to be alive." She'd say something like that, and probably drop her chalk, maybe let out a little scream, and maybe her eyes would fill with tears. Sometimes when she read a sad poem that happened, and she'd say what a wonderful poem it was. And none of the kids would laugh, just look serious, because they all liked old Tolson the vestal virgin.

Leaving the trenching tool, I backed out of the tunnel and climbed slowly down the shaft.

I wished I still had the candle to heat some warm water to sip so I wouldn't feel like my stomach was sticking to my backbone. I left the ceiling light on; I'd left the light on in the shaft. I didn't know why. I wished I'd had a chance to be a better person for the rest of my life, really repent like you're supposed to, and do all those things I'd planned to do. Like get my driver's license, buy a car, have a girlfriend, really get to know Frank, go on a mission, even become spiritual, go to college and have Mark as a roommate, become an engineer or something, get married, make love, have kids, even learn to play the piano. Closing my eyes, I saw Frank and Lucille and everybody, saw our house with the Christmas tree all lit up, my room, the neighborhood, everything.

Nate and Clay both told me what it was like getting out of the MTC and being on the plane flying to your mission. Sitting in your seat, you look down at your name tag because you know now you're a real missionary. And the lady sitting next to you asks if you are one, and you say yes ma'am, and she says, "Tell me all about your church. I've heard it's a wonderful church. I listen to your Tabernacle Choir every Sunday." Your hands trembling, you reach for your scriptures, closing your eyes just for that second, praying harder than you've ever prayed in your life that you'll be all inspired and remember at least something you learned in the MTC. First you ask the lady where she's from, has she been visiting in Salt Lake, does she have any Mormon friends, has she enjoyed herself—buttering her all up like they teach you. And then you open your triple combination to the description of the First Vision and say, "The Prophet Joseph Smith . . ."

I opened my eyes. I was really sorry they would find me like this next spring, all frozen like the guy in the glacier, but I'd done all I could, worked hard, figured things out, had faith. You just had to accept the Lord's will, like Trace did I guess, which is what Lucille always said, even though you might want to talk to someone later and ask why it was all necessary. Just to be sure it wasn't a mistake or something, and you might get to go back to Earth, which everybody would think was a miracle or something. I didn't think Lucille would be in any big hurry to have my memorial service because she didn't want to think of me dead, all frozen and stiff under the avalanche, and they'd have to convince her.

"Lucille, Kyle's been gone for nearly two weeks. We need to make plans for his service."

"I know, I know. I just can't believe he's gone. How can he be gone? He's only fifteen."

"Darling, be reasonable, please."

"I don't want to be reasonable. Why should I be reasonable? I've already lost one son."

"Darling, we have to meet with Bishop Goodmer to make the arrangements."

Lucille would just sit there; she wouldn't say anything.

I wanted to be buried next to Grandpa and Grandma Hooper and Trace in the family plot. It was okay. I'd have a headstone just like Trace, with my full name and the dates I was born and died. Lucille would bring fresh flowers every week in the summer, like she did for Trace. It would be sort of interesting meeting all those dead people you knew or had heard about. Thinking about it didn't bother me much anymore because I'd be with my family. I wondered what nice things they'd say about me in my obituary, because they'd have to put one in the *Silver City Herald* finally and have a service, although I knew that Mom still wouldn't want to. I hoped Summer would remember me a little bit. Even when she was out on a date with some guy, she'd wish it was me, and be sad. I was sorry Lucille would have to clean out all my stuff and take it to Good Will.

• • •

I pushed the quilt off, reached over, and got an old envelope and a pencil out of the glove compartment. I'd decided to write a note telling everybody how sorry I was. But then I didn't feel like writing all that. I had to make a fist to hold the pencil and write in big awkward letters: "I tried. See you all later. I'll say hello to Grandma and Grandpa Hooper and Trace for you. I love everybody. Kyle." I liked that. Miss Tolson would like it too; I didn't think it had any punctuation, grammar, or spelling errors, and no unnecessary words. I hoped Lucille would give the school one of my skiing pictures for the "In Memoriam" page at the back of the yearbook. I put the note on the passenger seat.

I looked at myself one last time in the rearview mirror. My face was really thin, dirty, gray, one side still streaked with dry blood, my long hair matted where it stuck out from my hat and hood; dark-rimmed, my eyes sunk deep back in my head like I was a hundred years old. I didn't turn off the light. What was the point now? I'd just let it grow dimmer and dimmer until I was just sitting there in the darkness, the quilt pulled up to my chin, not even needing to open my eyes.

I lay back in the seat, knew that everything was darkness outside the Suburban, except the light at the end of the shaft, but then the battery would die and the lights would all go out. The darkness didn't scare me anymore. I wondered what would happen when I actually died. Did you really see a light or somebody all dressed in white coming toward you, maybe Trace because he was your brother, which would be sort of nice? I wasn't afraid, just tired. I didn't ever want to move again. I knew dying wouldn't be painful. I'd fall asleep and just wouldn't wake up. That's what happened when you were freezing and dying of hypothermia.

I wanted everybody to know how hard I'd tried, that I was that kind of kid. But I knew too that as the avalanche melted, the cave and the shaft would vanish. Maybe everything would just cave in. So nobody would know, except they'd find the light wire, the pop-can exhaust hose, and all the limbs I'd sawed through, and figure out what that meant and say, "What a brave kid." Maybe. They would find my body in the seat. I smiled at that. Things didn't always work out the way you wanted. I was sorry about a lot of things, but that was okay. I knew now that was the way life was sometimes. Except I really would have liked to be clean when they found me, not so dirty. I didn't like to say "found my body." I was still me, at least for a while. I hoped that Lucille would give Mark something to remember me by, maybe my mountain bike.

"Grandpa Hooper."

I spoke Grandpa's name just once, like we were back in the cabin and I wanted something. I knew Grandma and Grandpa would be waiting for me, and Trace too because he was my brother, which I knew was having faith and being spiritual, a little anyway. I just wanted to be with them, wanted to see them off in the distance and walk toward them, Trace and Grandma hugging me, Grandpa giving me one of those big bear hugs of his and then handing me a sucker. I didn't know what they would do afterward. I didn't care. I would just be with them, probably in a house somewhere, sleeping in the same bedroom with Trace, who would be all healed and strong again. I hoped they had suckers in heaven. I couldn't imagine why not, if heaven was a place where you were supposed to be happy. There might even be girls in heaven. There'd have to be, wouldn't there? And maybe Grandma Hooper, who was a great cook, would make this big welcome supper with roast beef and potatoes and gravy and apple pie and everything.

"Trace."

I knew why I said Trace's name, because now I understood what Trace had to go through two weeks before he slipped into a coma, why he cried, because he wasn't going to get a chance to live his life. But he had faith; Grandpa and Grandma had come to help, kind of welcomed him I guess. And thinking about that, I felt a rich, warm feeling for Trace, who was my big brother and really was a great person who died.

"Man, Trace, man. I'm so sorry."

And I started to cry, not sobbing or anything like that, but just crying, not feeling the tears slipping down my cold cheeks, but looking down and seeing them dropping on the

quilt. I knew I wasn't crying just for Trace or myself, but for
everybody, especially for my mom, not Lucille, but my mom
because that's what she was, and Frank was my dad. But crying
was all right because I'd done everything I could do, tried to
figure things out, think, hadn't sat around on my butt, just like
my Grandpa Hooper said you shouldn't. I'd had faith in God
and Jesus. Even men cried sometimes, even soldiers in Korea.
I'd found out what kind of person I really was. I wasn't so bad,
I didn't think. Not inestimable I guess, but sort of worthy. I
kind of liked myself, having faith and everything.

After a while I wiped my eyes on my parka sleeve and just
sat there not worrying about anything anymore, just listening
to Crystal Creek. When I was maybe six, maybe five, Grandpa
Hooper took me fishing for the first time and let me pull in
my first trout. Grandpa liked to fish Crystal Creek in the late
afternoon when the tall spruces going up the slope at the far
end of the basin shaded everything, the whole south side of the
basin covered in spruces.

After we caught our limit, Grandpa took me by the hand
and we climbed up into the spruces and just sat there in the
cool afternoon shade watching the squirrels and chipmunks.
Grandpa always brought a pocketful of peanuts for me to feed
them. Grandpa pulled down the flat, green limbs to show me
how to identify a spruce and pay attention to details. Grandpa
was always telling me to do that. The whole south end of the
bowl was a wall of beautiful blue-green spruces.

In the dim half-circle of light from inside the Suburban
and the light from the shaft, I saw the mink standing on a log,
a small trout in its mouth. And then it was gone, just like last
time, a small, black moving shadow vanishing. I sat up slowly.
One afternoon as I sat with my grandfather in the cool spruce
shade, we saw a mink climb a spruce tree and walk out on
one of the flat, horizontal limbs, probably hunting a squirrel or
maybe a chipmunk.

As I sat there waiting to slowly freeze to death but hoping the mink would come back one last time, my eyes half-closed, I understood something. Understood it slowly, but like something I'd earned, partly anyway, something I was entitled to know.

The wall of limbs I'd run into weren't broken off, not a huge tangle of broken spruce limbs. They were the limbs of standing spruce trees, flat, horizontal limbs, the trees on the south side of the bowl. The avalanche, its energy gone, had crossed Crystal Creek, run up the hill, hit the side of the bowl, and stopped.

I sat there in the dim light thinking about what that new knowledge meant, and I knew I still had a chance, and maybe that Lucille wouldn't have to lose me too, like Trace, maybe.

"Thank you, Grandpa Hooper. Thank you too, God." I didn't know how you thanked the Holy Ghost. I'd never heard of anybody doing that. But I was grateful anyway. I knew he'd helped me understand because that's what he was supposed to do.

I pushed back the quilt. I climbed out of the Suburban. I did everything slowly, without strength. I wasn't excited. I just knew I still had a chance. If only I'd known I could have cut a horizontal tunnel right into the spruces, but there was no way I could have known how far the avalanche went before it stopped. I couldn't know everything. I still didn't know how far the avalanche went into the spruces and I didn't have a light to dig by. I knew I had to climb a standing spruce to get out.

Slowly I climbed the shaft and into the tunnel. I crawled past the light toward the exposed limbs; my bow saw and trenching tool lay on the floor of the tunnel.

Doing everything by feel in the darkness, I pushed the snow away from the limbs with the trenching tool. The snow was loose, not packed hard. Leaving stubs to climb on, I cut off limbs, pushing the snow and cut limbs out of the way. If the top of the spruce stuck out of the avalanche, I had a chance. If not, that's where they'd find me, like a big frozen squirrel in a tree. I smiled. In the spring when they didn't find me in the Suburban, they'd wonder where I was.

My hands were numb, frostbitten, my gloves shreds. I had to be careful not to cut my hands when I sawed each limb off. I wouldn't feel it. The snow was looser back in the limbs. The growing numbness in my feet went almost to my knees. I didn't need to wipe off my goggles; I couldn't see anything anyway. I wore them just for protection.

I hit the trunk of the spruce with the blade of the trenching tool. I put out my hands to feel the trunk, felt it with the back of my hand because my fingers were dead. There wasn't much snow now, but the limbs were still too dense to climb up through. I had to cut a path. I dropped the trenching tool. I didn't need it anymore.

Exhausted, I worked very slowly and totally by feel in the darkness. I had to be careful. If I cut myself badly, I could bleed to death and not even know it was happening.

I felt with my wrists and forearms. I was so weak I had to stop two or three times cutting off one limb. The limbs didn't fall; they just hung in the loose, frozen snow. I pushed them aside. I had to remember to leave a stub to climb on. Had to keep thinking, play it smart. In the darkness I wrapped my left arm around the trunk, so I wouldn't fall. I was deep in the icy spruce limbs, the limbs from the surrounding trees pushing in.

"I can't do it anymore. I can't. I just can't."

I had both arms over limbs. I hung there.

"I can't is a sucker who won't try."

I sawed off the next limb and slowly pulled myself up. I cut off another limb and rested. I took longer and longer rests. The limbs were getting smaller, the trunk tapering a little. If the top of the spruce wasn't out of the snow, I was toast. I smiled. Toast. I sawed off another limb, pushing and pulling, then resting, pushing and pulling, resting. I hung by my arms, my forehead pressed against the trunk.

The air was cooler on my numb face.

I cut another limb. I knew I couldn't cut anymore. I cut one more limb. I stuck my head in the open space.

I pushed my goggles up on my forehead. Looking out through the space where the limb had been, I saw something that wasn't darkness. I blinked my eyes. I looked. I closed my eyes. I opened them. I saw sky. Stars. The moon. Under the darker sky I saw white mountain peaks.

I didn't speak. I kept looking at the sky, stars, moon, the white peaks. I was at the far side of the bowl, the slope spreading away at chest level, everything white, except the sky. I understood. I didn't have any words, at first.

I whispered, "Thank you. Thank you. Thank you."

I started to cry again, the tears slow and easy.

Dropping the bow saw, I crawled out on the mat of limbs frozen in the snow. I tried to stand up, but fell down on my face. Using my elbows and forearms, I pushed myself up on all fours. Kneeling, balancing with my arms held out, I stood up. My hands and feet were gone. I stood there.

Turning, I saw the Christmas lights of the lodge far up above the east side of the bowl and, above that, cabin lights. No night skiers because it was Christmas Eve. I turned back. I saw the lights of a car coming down the Silver Canyon road, the lights just a moving glow above the wall of plowed snow. The road was closer.

Holding my arms out in front of me and to the side, tipping forward, I took one step and then the next and the next. I kept falling. I hit my forehead on something hard. Pushing up on my elbows and knees, I saw blood dripping in the snow. Head hanging down, I crawled. The slope got steeper by the road, a bank of snow. I kept thinking how happy everybody would be to see me again and know I wasn't dead. I knew they would be happy. My mom would be happy. She'd help me.

Climbing the bank of piled snow by the road, I rolled back twice. When I got to the top the third time, I hung there and then rolled to the bottom by the road. I pushed myself to my knees. I was on a pull-off. I watched a car pass. The headlights didn't hit me. I was too far back. I stood up and staggered toward the road.

Another car came down the road. The headlights hit me, but the car didn't stop. A third car came. When the lights hit me, I fell to my knees. "Please." The car passed me, but then I heard it stop. I turned my head. The car was backing up, the tail lights casting a red glow across the snow.

I saw a face close to the door window. The window came down.

"You all right, son?"

I looked at the man.

"Something wrong?"

"I need to go home." Pushing with my hands I got up on one foot, then slowly stood up.

"You been drinking? Speak louder. I can't hear you."

"I need to go home. My mom's worried."

I saw the man bend to reach over to the glove compartment. He opened the door and got out. He shined the flashlight on me.

"You look awful, son. What have you been doing? Do you know your head's bleeding? You looked starved."

"Will you take me home, mister, please. My mom." I spoke slowly.

"Who are you? What's your name, son?"

"My name is Kyle, Kyle Frank Hooper."

"You're who?"

"Kyle Frank Hooper. I'm Kyle Frank Hooper."

"Oh, come on. This isn't Halloween; it's Christmas Eve.

That Hooper boy's been under that avalanche for over a week. What are you trying to pull, anyway? You're drunk."

I sagged forward. I felt the man catch me and lower me to the snow.

I looked up at the man's face.

"I got out."

"Out of where?"

"The snow."

"The avalanche? Son, that's impossible. It's been nine days."

I lifted up my right hand. The ends of the fingers sticking through the shredded glove were black with frostbite. The man pushed my hood back. He shined the flashlight in my face.

"Grandpa Hooper's Suburban . . . a tank, a big spruce on top . . . dug a tunnel."

"It's not possible. Miracles don't . . ."

"Will you take me home, mister? My mom."

"Oh my good hell. We better get you to a hospital. You're in bad shape."

"Go home."

I felt the man lift me to my feet and half-carry me around to the passenger side of the car. He opened the door and lowered me onto the seat, lifted my feet into the car. He reached across me and fastened the seat belt. He got in and closed the door. The engine was running. I felt the warmth from the heater.

"I'll call your folks to meet us at the hospital. Can you remember your number?"

"No. Need to go home. Don't want to upset my family. My mom. Home. Please."

"All right, son. All right. What's your address? But you need to get to a hospital. Sheriff Catchwell needs to know about this."

I felt the beginning pain in my frostbitten fingers from the heat.

The man dialed three numbers on his speaker phone.

"Is this an emergency?" I heard a woman's voice ask.

"I need the sheriff's office. No, you can't help me. I need the sheriff's office. Yes, this is an emergency. No. Just give me his office. I know Sheriff Catchwell. Thank you."

The man pulled out onto the road.

"Sheriff's office."

"This is an emergency. Is Sheriff Catchwell there?"

"The sheriff is just leaving to go home. It's Christmas Eve. We had a major freeway pileup. May I help you?"

"No. Give me Sheriff Catchwell."

"I'm sure I could—"

"Get Sheriff Catchwell back. Get him back. Tell him it's Jim Freely. He knows me. This is an emergency."

I looked out the windshield, clenched my jaws against the growing pain.

"Sheriff Catchwell."

"Jack? Jack, this is Jim Freely. You're not going to believe what I'm going to tell you, but believe it anyway. I'm driving down Silver Canyon. I've got the Hooper boy in the car. He's alive. He's in terrible shape, starved, but he's alive. His fingers are all frostbitten. I just picked him up at that pull-off above the bowl. He dug himself out."

"Jim, you've been celebrating too much. That Hooper boy's been buried for nine days."

I kept clenching my jaws.

"No, Jack, I know it's Christmas Eve. I know it's impossible. It's him. It's Kyle Hooper. I didn't believe it either. It's like he rose from the dead. But it's him, Jack. He dug himself out. That big Suburban saved him. Call it a miracle, call it whatever you want, but I know a boy named Kyle Hooper is in my car and I'm driving down Silver Canyon."

"That's not possible, Jim. How could he do that?"

I watched car lights coming toward us. My hands were on fire. My feet were starting to hurt.

"Don't ask me how. I don't know how. All I know is that the Hooper boy is in my car and I'm headed down Silver Canyon. He wants to go home first. He insists on that, to see his mom. Didn't want me to phone his folks. Doesn't want to worry them. I told him I'd take him."

"Well, what kind of shape is he in then, if he's there in your car like you say?"

"Frostbite, looks starved, dirty. Got a bad cut on his head. He's awfully weak. He's in a lot of pain."

"All right, I'll meet you at Silver Canyon Junction."

"Okay, okay. I'll meet you at the junction. Good. I'm almost out of the canyon now. Good."

The man clicked off his phone.

"You heard it, son. Sheriff Catchwell is going to meet us at the junction."

I watched two more cars coming up the canyon.

"You okay? You going to make it?"

I nodded.

"You want it warmer?"

I shook my head. "Hurts."

I saw the Silver City lights at the mouth of the canyon. The man kept turning to look at me and shaking his head.

"Son, you're a hero. You deserve a medal."

The traffic got heavier. I saw three police cars with lights flashing pulled over to the side of the road. The cops stood by the cars. The man pulled over.

Three cops in Smokey Bear hats walked back toward us. The man lowered my window. A short, heavy cop bent down. Sheriff Catchwell. I turned toward him. He shined a flashlight in my face. He turned off the flashlight, stood bent down looking at me.

"Okay, it's the Hooper kid all right. I've seen him before a couple of times, as I recall. I don't know how it's him. But it is. Every once in a while you see things in this job that can't happen. Kind of nice for a change."

"I couldn't believe it when I picked him up. Makes you want to cry when you think of his family. What a Christmas present."

"Well, let's get him down there. We need to get to a hospital as quick as we can. Better see his mom first, I guess. It's on the way. I'll have an ambulance at the house. We'll block the boulevard. You follow me. You said you didn't phone his folks?"

"He didn't want me to. Afraid it would upset his mom."

"Upset his mom? Well, I don't think she ever really believed her boy was dead. Women are strange. Lots of faith we men don't know anything about, I guess. We'll turn off the sirens after we cross the boulevard. No point in terrifying the whole neighborhood." Sheriff Catchwell reached in and put his hand on my shoulder. "I hear the neighbors on your folks' street haven't turned on their outside Christmas lights because of you, son. Kind of thoughtful."

Sheriff Catchwell and the other two cops walked back to their cars.

I watched the flashing lights and heard the sirens as we crossed Wayne Boulevard.

The sheriff turned onto Blackfoot Drive. The sirens stopped, the flashing red and blue lights casting shadows on the snow. I saw the familiar houses. Lit Christmas trees stood in the front windows, the outside house Christmas lights not lit.

I saw Sheriff Catchwell stop in front of my house, the windows lit. I saw him walk up to my house. The three cop cars with their flashing lights lit up the street. They'd pulled ahead so Mr. Freely could park in front of my house. The other two cops got out. Neighbors came out of their houses to stand on their front porches, hugging themselves against the cold.

My window rolled down. I saw our front door open, Sheriff Catchwell silhouetted against the light. He turned and pointed toward the car. He kept pointing and talking. I saw my mom and my dad come out on the porch and stop. Nate, Clay, Brooke, and Jed came out. My dad lifted his arm from around my mom's shoulders, Sadie jumping up and down in front of them barking. My mom walked down the steps, and then she ran. Mr. Freely opened the car door.

My mom stood looking at me. She didn't say anything. She reached in and brushed the hair back out of my eyes.

"Oh, Kyle. I knew. I knew." My mom kept saying my name over and over. "You're alive, you're alive." She kept stroking my face. She held my hands. She kissed my hands. "Oh, Kyle. Oh, Kyle. They said we'd lost you."

I saw my dad's face in the doorway. I heard Nate yelling that it was me, and I was alive. The neighbors shouted, whistled, waved their arms, and turned to hug each other.

Sadie shoved her head in.

"Hello, girl."

I saw Sheriff Catchwell. "I think we'd better get this boy to the hospital as quick as we can, Mr. Hooper. The ambulance is here."

My dad put his hands on my mom's shoulders and helped her straighten up. She was shaking and crying. Clay and Nate each put an arm through one of Mom's.

My dad reached in and undid my seat belt.

"How you doing, son?"

"Okay, Dad."

Dad reached in, took me in his arms, and lifted me out of Mr. Freely's car. Turning, holding me tight against him, he laid me on the gurney. The paramedics covered me with a blanket. My dad bent and kissed me.

"You're going to be okay, son."

"I know."

I saw Brooke and Jed standing by Mom, Clay, and Nate. I wanted Trace to be standing there too. Brooke hadn't had her baby yet. I saw the front yard and street full of neighbors. They'd gone all quiet, and then they began to clap and shout and whistle and hug each other again. I saw Mark standing with his mom. Mark gave me the thumbs up.

The paramedics lifted my gurney into the ambulance. Dad helped Mom get in the ambulance. He sat with his arm around her.

"God helped me, Mom, and Jesus I think. And the Holy Ghost. Grandpa Hooper too. I had faith, Mom. I used my head."

She nodded. She reached out and put both hands on my arm. "I know. I know."

Dad smiled at me.

"Oh, Kyle, your hands. Your poor hands. Your face." Mom began to cry again.

I didn't say anything. My head turned, I saw out the window the Christmas lights coming on all along our street. I saw Nate shaking hands with Mr. Freely, then Nate hugging him.

• • •

I was in the hospital two weeks. My dad stayed with me every night the first week. He wouldn't let Mom stay. She was too worn out from all the worrying. When I'd wake up at night I'd see my dad sitting by the bed, his head resting on the edge, his hand on my arm. I'd see him, feel his hand, and I'd close my eyes, pray sort of because I was so grateful to be alive and live my life, and then I'd go back to sleep.

They didn't have to cut off any of my fingers or toes because of the frostbite. Doctor Wellmen said the ends of my fingers would be numb for a while. He said that my mom had told him that I played the piano; he said that would be great exercise for my fingers.

I wonder why that didn't surprise me.

Except for Mark, visitors could only be family. They wouldn't even let the TV people come to interview me. Miss Tolson sent this nice card saying how happy everybody was that I was still alive and hadn't died. All the kids in the class signed it, the girls kissing it to leave their lipstick prints. Mark told me he was going to be baptized and that his mom thought it would be just what he needed, although she still didn't come to church.

"Baptized? What do you want to do that for?"

"I prayed for you all the time, and I started reading the Book of Mormon too just to show Jesus how serious I was. I finished it last week. I prayed about it. I just know it's true. I just felt so happy. It's such a great feeling. You should try it."

"I told you to be careful."

"I want you to baptize me."

"Me?"

"Yes, you."

"I can't do that."

"Yes, you can, after you're ordained a priest. You'll be sixteen. I checked in the Doctrine and Covenants."

"Oh just great. My best friend isn't even baptized yet and already he's quoting scripture."

"I want to go to the temple and be baptized for my dad, so he can be a member too. And we need to get our patriarchal blessings. Your mom told me all about that. She said you were planning on getting one but keep putting it off for some reason. It's a really spiritual thing to do."

"Oh, sure."

The blessing was okay though. I needed to know all the things God wanted me to do, and I knew I was going to need all the help I could get. I was going to have to get my Eagle too, I guessed. I'd made all those promises to God, but of course that's when I thought I was about to perish. Still, I'd made a deal. It would be so arduous earning all those merit badges, probably finishing the day before I left on my mission. Maybe I could con old Mark into getting his now that he was so righteous. It wouldn't be so bad working on it together. Mom would be so glad that all her four boys made Eagle. Did every kid in the Church have to have his name on an Eagle plaque in the foyer just to prove that Zion's youth were making it somehow? Probably.

Mom fixed it so the nurse let Summer come to visit me. Summer brought me some brownies.

"You must have been very brave, Kyle." Summer touched my bandaged hands.

"Oh, I was."

When Summer left she leaned over the bed and kissed me right on the lips. I closed my eyes for that one moment just to feel it better. At the door she turned and smiled.

"Get better fast, Kyle."

"Oh, I will." Such a lovely.

After Summer had gone, I lay there looking out the hospital window and thinking about all the benefits of being sixteen, especially being able to date hot girls all the time. I thought maybe Mom and Dad would give me a car for my birthday. I'd get at least two thousand dollars insurance for the Suburban, maybe more. I'd had to pay all the premiums, so it was my money legally. And I'd suffered so much and been so brave and they were so grateful I was still alive. I could give girls rides to school in the morning and back in the afternoon, and go on double dates with Mark, but sometimes just alone with the girl. And I'd take girls skiing, especially Summer, and other girls too, because I couldn't go steady until after my mission, of course. And I'd be a priest for two years before that, and I'd have to be a good example for Mark because he'd probably want to go on a mission, too. And I'd be a better person too, which I knew I had to be, obey all the commandments, or at least try harder to, get the old Eagle. I'd have to watch it so things didn't get too voluptuous on dates and things. Everything was going to be so worthy, sort of anyway I guess, but I knew it was going to take a lot of faith, just like Lucille, I mean Mom, always says.

About the Author

Douglas Thayer taught English at Brigham Young University, where he served as director of composition, chair of creative writing, associate department chair, and associate dean of humanities. Awards for his fiction include the Karl G. Maeser Creative Arts Award, Whitney Lifetime Achievement Award, Smith-Pettit Foundation Award for Outstanding Contribution to Mormon Letters, and the *Dialogue* Prize for Imaginative Literature. He is the author of the memoir *Hooligan: A Mormon Boyhood,* the novels *The Tree House, Summer Fire,* and *The Conversion of Jeff Williams,* and three collections of short stories: *Mr. Wahlquist in Yellowstone, Under the Cottonwoods,* and *Wasatch.* Thayer has been published in *Colorado Quarterly, Dialogue, Prairie Schooner, Irreantum,* and elsewhere. He is married to Donlu DeWitt; they have six children and numerous grandchildren.

www.ingramcontent.com/pod-product-compliance
Lightning Source LLC
Chambersburg PA
CBHW070121260626
47160CB00004B/1561